dare truth or promise

# dare
# truth or
# promise

paula boock

Houghton Mifflin Company
Boston 1999

*For Terry, with love—*
*and for all of those for whom it was too hard*

I began writing this book while the Writer in Residence at the Dunedin College of Education, and completed it with the help of a writing grant from Creative New Zealand. I am grateful to both institutions for their generosity.

I would also like to thank Sister Campion for lending her name; William Taylor and Renée for lending me courage and example; and Barbara Larson for the time, friendship, and faith.

First published by Longacre Press in 1997,
9 Dowling Street, Dunedin, New Zealand

The text of this book is set in 11-point Berkeley Oldstyle.

*Library of Congress Cataloging-in-Publication Data*

Boock, Paula.
Dare truth or promise / Paula Boock.
p.   cm.
Summary: Louie Angelo, a Woodhaugh High prefect who plans to be a lawyer, falls in love with a girl who lives in a pub and just wants to get through her exams so she can become a chef.
ISBN 0-395-97117-9
[1. Lesbians—Fiction. 2. Love—Fiction 3. Friendship—Fiction. 4. New Zealand—Fiction.]   I. Title.
PZ7.B64485Dar   1999
[Fic] — dc21    98-51981   CIP  AC

Printed in the United States of America
BP 10 9 8 7 6 5 4 3 2 1

# a kiwi glossary

**axolotl** salamander

**bonnet** car hood

**bottle store** liquor store

**broom** shrub with yellow flowers

**bursary** scholarship or grant

**caper** acrobatic leap

**chip** french fry

**crib** to steal or borrow

**cuppa** cup of tea

**dob** to tell on

**duchess** dressing table or dresser

**fair dinkum** the real thing, authentic

**fiddly** awkward to do

**flat** apartment

**flatting** living in an apartment

**flick** the brush-off

**fossick** rummage, search around

**Freezing Works** abattoir, slaughterhouse

**goolies** testicles

**karaka** tree native to New Zealand

**Kiwi** person from New Zealand

**ladybird-step** to take tiny steps

**loo** bathroom

**natty** neat, dapper

**netball** variation of basketball

**op shop** second-hand clothing shop

**pottle** small container

**prefect** senior pupil authorized to maintain discipline, a monitor

**raked** tiered

**ranch sliders** sliding glass doors

**rimu** tree native to New Zealand

**RSI** Repetitive Strain Injury

**seratone** Formica

**shouting** buying rounds of drinks

**snib** to bolt, lock

**spa** hot tub or jacuzzi

**spotty** having acne

**takeaway** fast-food restaurant

**tui** native New Zealand bird

**ute** utility vehicle or pick-up truck

**wag** to skip school

# louie

There was a moment, later, that was a lightning strike. But the first time Louie saw Willa she had just begun the coleslaw. She had poured the bucket of mayonnaise over the mountain of cabbage and carrot and had plunged her hands up to her elbows in the freezing cold mixture when they walked in.

Kevin presented Willa like a new car, smug; he steered her around the kitchen, hand pressed to her back, his eyes running over her face as if he were polishing the paintwork. Then he ran into Deirdre, and you could almost hear the brakes squeak.

"And here we are, where all the real work takes place!" he announced, and was greeted by a snort. "This is Deirdre, Deirdre this is Willa—as in Will-a, Won't-a, just a little joke there," (and a little squeeze, thought Louie) "—and this is Louie. Louie's an after-schooler like you, and she's going to show you the ropes, aren't you Louie?"

Willa had long red hair which she'd pulled back in a bushy ponytail. Her skin was pale and she looked awful in the regulation Burger Giant cap and apron. She moved away from Kevin to re-tie her apron, then turned to Louie.

"Hi," she said, with a grin.

"Hi."

1

The air stretched momentarily.

Deirdre thrust a pile of flattened chicken boxes into Kevin's arms. "You can take these on your way out."

Kevin wasn't wearing his apron, and he took a quick step back and held the boxes at arm's length as they began to dribble blood from the bottom corner.

"Oh, gross," he said. "Clean that up, will you," and he disappeared out the door, beneath the board that held a photograph of Deirdre grimacing at the world and announcing that she was the Burger Giant Employee of the Week.

Louie watched Willa turn and follow her to the sink. She didn't have that new girl, first day at school look at all. She simply stood and waited as Louie washed her hands under the tap.

"Everyone has a duty each night," Louie explained. "I'm on salads and preparation, Deirdre's on filling orders and Simone's serving. Kelly's coming in soon to help, and Kevin's *supposed* to be on the counter with Simone." She watched as Willa looked about her carefully. "You'll begin with me on preparation, because we're behind, but fill orders with Deirdre later. You can start on these dishes."

Willa was good. She'd never worked in a takeaways before but she knew how to place the tomato around the edges of the burger so it looked fuller than it was; she knew how to smear the relish see-through thin on the bun; she knew how to chop spring onions with the scissors, not the knife.

"You must have worked in a Burger Giant in a previous life," said Louie.

Willa shrugged. "I get a lot of practice at home."

The real surprise was Deirdre. Deirdre hated Burger Giant. She hated Kevin. And she hated new staff. She barked a couple of explanations at Willa early in the evening and after that Willa didn't have to ask her anything. Deirdre's face showed a begrudging respect for the new girl when Willa fetched a jar of gherkins from the shelves without having to ask and loosened the tight lid by running it under hot water. To Deirdre such domestic skills were worth a hundred of Louie's Shakespearian quotes. In fact the only time she had seemed impressed with Louie's academic abilities was last summer when she'd served a husky young German tourist and Louie had spoken in broken Deutsch to take his order, and wished him a Glückliche Weihnachten.

When Kevin returned to total the cash register, take the money and lock up, Willa was putting away the third load of dishes for the evening.

"All settled in?" he asked, sidling up and cornering her against the chip warmer. "You look like you belong here already. Here," he said, taking a giant sieve from her, "I'll give you a hand putting those away."

Just then Kelly bounced in from the counter clutching a canvas bag.

"All done," she announced, and handed the bag to Kevin. "The door's snibbed but I've left the cash totalling to you." Kelly had had her teeth capped last month and she delivered her best All-American smile to Kevin. "Simone left five minutes early cos it was so quiet, okay?" Without waiting for an answer she pulled her apron over her head. Kelly always seemed to perform this maneuvre with the utmost squirming and wriggling, and always right in front of Kevin.

Willa used the distraction to slip away with a container full of cutlery. Kelly, who watched a lot of soaps, pushed home her advantage with a protracted stretch which left Kevin face to mammary glands for at least five stupefying seconds.

"Aaahhh, what a night," she moaned, eyes closed. "I can't wait to slip into my little bed."

*"I am your spaniel; and Demetrius, The more you beat me, I will fawn on you,"* Louie quoted sweetly to the air.

"Hmm, yes, okay Kelly," said Kevin, trying to cough his voice back into control, "pop that bag upstairs on my desk, will you?" He put the sieve down on the bench and slipped across to Willa again. Louie and Deirdre exchanged looks. Kevin's new girl routine was truly sickening, but also a matter of some fascination. More could be told about their new colleague from her reaction to Kevin's come-ons than any test they could devise.

Kelly had disappeared through the white swing door that led to the stairs and offices. Kevin approached Willa, or rather Willa's bottom, as she was bent over sorting cutlery into containers under the bench.

It was a gift to Kevin. His vision of himself as a subtle, sensitive operator in matters of seduction never conflicted with such an opportunity. He reached out and patted the bottom. As Willa leapt up, he dextrously managed to turn her so they were standing front to front, his arm still around her waist.

"Why, Willa, there's no need to leap on me," he smarmed, then lifted his arms out wide. "I'm all yours!"

Louie and Deirdre looked on in horror as he laughed at his joke. "Seriously though," he continued—

"Seriously," Willa interrupted, and now Kevin saw the butcher's knife pointing at his groin, "If you touch me again, I'll cut off your goolies and sell 'em for chicken nibbles. Understood?"

The air stretched thin again, the two figures taut and surreal. Willa was magnificent, all flame and fury, her eyes fixed on Kevin's. Louie noticed that they were a light light blue, like opals, and they glittered. The combination of ferocity and composure in Willa's manner had an immediate effect on Kevin, and he backed away, hands up like a gangster held at gunpoint.

Louie knew immediately that she should have threatened to chop off Kevin's dangly bits months ago.

Willa had a dog called Judas. It was a German Shepherd and it was tied up by the loading dock behind Burger Giant.

"Get down, Judas," she said as the dog leapt and whined in greeting, sniffing the bag of leftovers Deirdre had given Willa. In two years Deirdre had never once offered leftovers to Louie.

"Is he yours?" asked Louie, who was undoing the chain on a mountain bike.

"Yes, of course he's mine. He goes everywhere with me." Willa let the dog off his rope and he bounded in a few circles then came back to Willa's side and looked up at her with expectant eyes.

"*Every time for you a little death,*" said Louie, pushing her bike over to Judas and giving him a pat.

"Pardon?"

"Absence. *The times we went away, every time for you a little death.* It's a poem, to a dog."

"Do you always quote poetry?"

Louie shrugged, and followed Willa and Judas through an alleyway onto the street. "I just remember things sometimes."

"You must have a photographic memory. I can't remember anything off by heart." Willa clicked her tongue at Judas who had taken off in the wrong direction. He weaved briskly back to Willa, nose sweeping the pavement for scents. "You going this way?" Willa asked Louie.

Louie paused. She did go that way, but was planning to ride her bike. Willa had already started walking, Judas trotting happily at her side. Louie wheeled her bike along the footpath to catch up. "Sure."

It had been raining, and the streetlights left a smear of yellow along George Street. They passed a few other people coming out of bars and restaurants, but mostly it was still and empty, and Louie had a strange urge to leap about in the middle of the road and shout out loud, to take possession of the main street of Dunedin.

"It's weird isn't it, no one in George Street," she said.

"Spooky," agreed Willa. "I love it late at night. It's my favourite time. Come on!" And she jumped onto the road and began running along the centre line, Judas loping beside her, tongue hanging out. "Race you!" she shouted, from a good head start. "To the horse!"

Louie swung a leg over her bike and started pedalling crazily, the bike lurching left and right as she tried to get up speed and overtake Willa. The tyres whizzed against the wet road and somewhere behind her the Town Hall clock began striking midnight.

"Aaaarrggh!" groaned Willa from ahead as she drew to a stop. Arthur Barnett's neon horse posted up and down on top of the shop roof like a lobotomised Davy Crockett minus his arms which had short-circuited. "Judas won," Willa panted to Louie as she caught up. The pale tip of Judas's tail could just be seen bouncing along the road ahead. "Oi! Judas! Get back here," she shouted, and the dog turned a wide circle and began trotting back along the road.

"You're fast," Louie commented. "For someone who's just worked seven hours."

"I like speed."

Louie decided she did too.

Willa went to Woodhaugh Girls' High too, but explained to Louie that she'd just moved there from Miller Park College, and was doing mostly repeat sixth form subjects. When Louie asked her why she'd shifted schools Willa laughed and said, "Did she jump or was she pushed? You should have a poem about that."

There was a person shuffling along the edge of the kerb, pulling things out of rubbish bins. Louie didn't know if it was a man or woman, they were so covered with layers of clothes and hung about with semi-filled plastic garbage bags. Both of them fell silent as they watched the figure sift through the nearest bin, undoing wrappers and sniffing chip packets. As they got closer Louie saw that it was a woman.

Judas trotted over to investigate. Willa called him but he only paused for a moment. When he reached the woman she made a strange noise and pulled the rubbish bags closer round her body. "Git! Git out!" She flapped a hand at the dog, and Judas jumped back and barked.

"Oh god," said Willa. She called out to Judas, but he was startled by the strange jerky movements of the woman, and kept barking at her. She bustled around the other side of the rubbish bin and hissed at him, which only made him more excited.

"Stop it, Judas," said Willa, going over to get him. Judas looked at Willa and barked a couple more times. "Sorry," she apologised. The woman turned her head away from Willa and didn't speak. She held on tight to her garbage bags. "Look," said Willa, "would you like these?" And she pulled out of her pack a Burger Giant bag. Judas jumped up at it as she held it out, but the woman turned further away.

"Bugger off!" she spat.

"Go on," said Willa. "They're leftovers, you might be able to use them. Please," she added, when the woman didn't respond.

"Put 'em in there." The woman fired the words like gunshot, flicking a hand at the rubbish bin and turning away again.

Willa walked over to the bin and placed the bag carefully on the top. Judas tried to jump up at it, but she said "No" firmly, and then kept him at heel as she walked back to where Louie stood. The woman never moved. Louie made a face at Willa.

"Come on," Willa replied, frowning. "Keep moving."

For the second time that night, Louie admired Willa's behaviour. Why didn't she ever have the poise to offer something to tramps instead of just feeling bad? Louie hopped back on her bike and paddled it along with her feet beside Willa.

"That stuff with Kevin," she said, trying not to make a big deal of it, "that was cool."

Willa gave a little sniff, and scuffed a stone in front of her. They were both on the pavement now.

"You reckon?"

"Yeah. He had it coming to him. I wish I'd done it ages ago." Louie mentally kicked herself for saying so much.

Willa turned her head and looked up at Louie, a delighted smile like a new moon on her face.

"I guess I won't be Employee of the Week, eh?"

As they approached the Duke Street intersection they hit another bunch of people spilling out onto the street. Three men had their arms around each other, singing, "Love me tender, love me do, all my dreams come trewww..." Someone else yelled out from a ute, "Seeya in sexual. Seeyin Sexual Targa," by which Louie worked out he meant Central Otago. She was just about to tell Willa what she thought he'd said, when her companion stopped and called Judas to heel again.

"Home sweet home."

Louie looked about. There was only a park, a bus terminal, a service station and—

"The pub?"

"Uhuh," grunted Willa. "We live upstairs." She waited till the ute did a U-turn and roared off down the street. "See ya, Louie," she said, as she and Judas crossed the road.

"See ya," replied Louie, still startled. She half-lifted a hand. "Maybe at school, eh?"

"Yeah, maybe."

Louie stared at the pub. It was a big concrete building painted dark green and red, a neon sign outside advertising it as the DB Duke Tavern. The bottle store and lounge bar were both dark, but there was a light on somewhere in the public bar. Upstairs three long narrow windows were lit behind blinds like yellow teeth.

Louie looked back to the street to see which door Willa had gone in, but there was no sign of her or Judas.

# willa

Willa was first up in the morning again. She wasn't used to it. Bliss always used to be in the bathroom hogging the shower or stealing Willa's hairdryer then singing at the top of her voice.

She made herself toast and tea, and took a cup through to her mother.

Jolene stirred when Willa turned on the radio, and then she spotted the tea beside her.

"Oh, you wee love," she croaked, and pulled herself up in bed to drink it.

The morning light was a cold winter glare through the upstairs window as Willa drew back the curtains and rolled up the old manila blind. Through the bars of the fire escape she watched the early traffic bunch up at the lights, then take off in a cloud of exhaust. The mechanic at the corner service station stood over the open bonnet of an old Cortina as his friend revved the engine and added more exhaust to the morning air.

"Pass me m' smokes, love."

Willa turned and studied her mother.

"Don't start. I've got a bloody shocker." Jolene leaned her head back against the headboard and closed her eyes. Willa tossed a full packet of cigarettes and a lighter from the dresser. They landed on Jolene's lap, and she patted the bedclothes until she located them. Jolene always had headaches in the morning these days, and she seemed to have given up trying to quit smoking. "You bloody try to quit smoking while you're working in it all day," she'd say. "It's like Jenny Craig working in a flamin' cake shop."

Willa perched on the dresser and watched as her mother lit the cigarette and drew in deeply. "Ahh, beaut. That's better." The line of white smoke she exhaled flowed toward the window where it mingled with the dirty white view. Jolene reached for her cup of tea with one hand and the ashtray beside her bed with the other. Her hair was muzzed on the side where she'd been sleeping and her face was blotched with pink on that side too. Her eyes looked small and bare in her face without make-up.

"Oh, god love, don't look at me, I'm a mess," she said, catching Willa's eye, and with the hand that held the cigarette she tugged away at the flatter side of her hair. Jolene had the same red hair as her two daughters, but nowadays she dyed it a darker auburn to cover the greying temples.

"No one looks good in the morning, Mum." Willa stepped inside an approaching drift of cigarette smoke, and flopped into an old armchair on the other side of the bed.

"You all ready for school?" her mother asked.

"Just need some money for lunch."

Jolene snorted. "Shoulda known. Cups of tea don't come cheap round here." She pointed at the dresser. "In me handbag. Oh, there's the mail there too, from yesterday. I think there's a letter from Bliss and Gary. Bring it over. You got time?" she asked her daughter.

"Sure, if you've got the money." Willa dropped the black bag into her mother's hands.

"You've lived in a pub too long." Jolene rummaged in her purse and pulled out a note. "That enough?" she asked Willa.

"Uhuh." She put it in the pocket of her jeans and sat back down in the armchair. Jolene was sorting through a bundle of letters, firing the bills onto her bedside table and putting others beside her on the bed. She handed one to Willa with a grin. "Love letter?" she quipped. Then she frowned quickly and bit her lip. "Just joking," she muttered and returned to her own mail. "Here it is," she said with relief, and looked back at her daughter. Willa's letter had disappeared.

"Open it," Willa replied.

The letter was in Bliss's large round writing. She and Gary had found a flat in Grey Lynn, nice and central, although it was a bit of a hovel. They were sharing with two other guys, an ex-girl-friend of one and occasionally her new boyfriend. "Nice going," commented Willa. Gary was loving his mate's workshop, lots of grunty bikes and good overtime, and Bliss had just got a part-time job in a clothes shop in Newmarket. The weather was fantastic, still shirt-sleeves, they'd heard it was freezing in Dunedin at the moment blah blah blah . . . Hope the pub's okay and no hassles lately, make sure Sid looks after you all right, and love to Willa, tell her to stay out of my wardrobe I still want those things, hope everything's good at the new school, what a business—Jolene faltered a bit in her reading.

"You told her." Willa glowered at her mother.

"Only a little, love."

"What does she say?"

"Oh, not much, just the usual." Jolene turned the page.

"What?"

Jolene sighed and turned back. "She just says it sounds like an overreaction to her."

"Huh. That's for real." Willa got up and started to leave the room.

"You fed Judas?" Jolene asked.

"Yup."

"Elvis?"

"No, not yet." Willa tried to close the door.

"Do it before you leave."

Elvis chirped as soon as Willa came back into the kitchen, and Judas bounced around her legs.

"Okay, okay," she said irritably. She took the feeding dishes out of the birdcage and washed them in the sink. She hated the sweet smell of the budgie cage, and the mixture of droppings and white fluff that always got in the water dish. As she replaced the filled dishes in his cage, Elvis jumped back and forth from his perch to his swing to the bars of the cage and chirrupped at Willa.

"Yeah yeah," she muttered, sliding down the glass plates that held the dishes in place. "Life's a dream, I know."

When Willa picked up a shoulder bag that held all her school work from the table, Judas jumped up and ran to the door with her.

"Sorry mate," she said, patting the dog's head. "I'll see you after school." Judas's ears flattened and he stretched his lowered head out toward the door hopefully. "You know the story, Judas," Willa warned, and the big dog sank to the floor and gazed up at her with his sad brown eyes. Willa gave him a last rub around the ears which made him thump his tail once only, then she went out the door and headed for the stairs. She yelled a "Hooray" to her mother, but all she could hear in reply was a hacking cough from the bedroom.

At the turn of the stairs she hit the smell. Beer. The smell of it and cigarettes pervaded her life. The walls of the pub seemed to ooze it, and although Jolene and Sid were scrupulous about cleaning up at night, not the morning after, the smell never disappeared. At the bottom of the stairs she glanced through the glass doors to the lounge bar. The red and gold patterned carpet was in shadow but a little light from the window made the dark wood tables and stalls gleam and the spirit bottles glittered from above the bar. Willa reached into her back pocket and pulled out the pale blue letter her mother had handed her. She stared at it for a bit, then finally ripped it open, and read the slip of paper inside.

*Die, bitch.*

Woodhaugh Girls' High was set in a small open valley in north Dunedin, an area which had become popular in recent years with the subdivision of a tract of land along Woodhaugh, high on the sunny side. New residents had fabulous views to the north of the city across hills of native bush—much of which had been felled on their side in order to build houses. The Leith River ran through the heart of the gorge, and spread around its course was the original valley suburb known for its modest homes, bush tracks, gardens and a park. During summer it could be idyllic, but winter in the valley was harsh and the new residents on top of the hill often looked down on a blanket of fog and permafrost where the park and the school were located.

It was a short walk for Willa from the Duke to the new brick school in the valley. The sleek, colourful classrooms, albeit over-heated by eight o'clock in the morning, were a luxury compared to the old prefabs at Miller Park. These were carpeted, and had comfortable chairs and soundproofed rooms. All she could re-member from Miller Park was noise—constant clatter and sound rebounding off thin, shiny walls.

The hall was really an auditorium, with raked blue seating looking down on a wide polished wood stage. At assembly Willa's form filled about two rows on the left of the hall. The principal, Mrs. Eagles, spoke to them about the usual things; the debating team had won something, the Maori Culture Group was going to Turangawaewae, the netball team was fund-raising, nobody was returning their library books and studies had shown smokers didn't make it to the top one third of management. Mrs. Eagles called it the "nicotine ceiling" and some girls laughed. Willa knew all about nicotine ceilings, but she thought she was probably taking it too literally.

The prefects sat at the front of the auditorium facing the stage, and Mrs. Eagles gestured to the front row, then called up Louise Angelo to speak about drama.

Louie was dressed as a clown in spotted pantaloons and a crazily patterned shirt. She wore huge pink plastic shoes which she fought with getting up the steps to the stage. When the audience began to laugh, she played it up, and fell over, then glared at Mrs. Eagles who was laughing at her. Finally she waddled to the microphone, patted it, then got a big fright when the thump reverberated around the hall. She went back slowly and blew in it and the same thing happened. Eventually, pretending to be terrified by the audience and the mike, she read her lines from dozens of tiny little cue cards in the flattest, dullest voice you could imagine.

"Ladies and gentlemen it. Is my pleasure to invite you. To the magnificent stupid — stupi — stupendous unbelievably exciting. Opening of the Comedy Club." Her face was unmoving and she continued in the same frightened-to-death voice. "Today at lunchtime right. Here in the auditorium you will. Never forget the thrill. And spectacle of our performance everyone. Is welcome but please — do. Not get too excited. Tickets are free yes. Free from the prefects. Room you must have a ticket to get. In get yours now yes now and laugh your heads. Off at the wit brilliance and. Antics of the world's funniest comedy troupe from Woodhaugh. High." Then Louie turned to Mrs. Eagles with relief and as the principal congratulated her on getting through it she pretended to faint in Mrs. Eagles' arms. A few wry slaps on the cheeks from Mrs. Eagles brought the clown around pretty quickly, and holding her hurt cheeks she shambled off the stage to a round of applause and laughter from the school.

Next to her, a girl Willa had met last week, Geena, said, "She's so good, eh. Got anything on at lunchtime?"

Willa shook her head.

"Let's go then, eh?" Geena had dark hair and a cheeky grin. "Should be a laugh."

"As long as there's no audience participation," answered Willa. "I like plays where I sit and know I'm safe."

"Scaredy-cat." They were moving out of the hall. "What've you got now?" Geena asked.

"Maths."

"Who?"

"Mrs. Lamont."

Geena grimaced. "Better you than me. Okay," she said, as they came to an intersection of corridors and got caught in the press, "I've got a free, I'll pick up tickets for both of us and meet you — where? Here?"

"Sure!" yelled Willa as Geena was swept further away. "Twelve-twenty, here!"

15

# willa

The tickets to the Comedy Club performance were bright orange with the letters PCC on them. At the door to the auditorium they were checked but everyone was told to hold onto them. Geena and Willa found seats right at the front, which was lucky because the auditorium was about two-thirds full.

Eventually the lights went out and Willa noticed a large screen on the stage.

"Did you ever hear the one about..." came a voice through the auditorium speakers

"...the *teacher*???" On the screen appeared a huge face shoved up against the camera so it was distorted and ugly. One beady eye peered out at the audience.

A person jumped out from behind the stage. "She resigned from the morgue because of too much talking back."

Another figure leapt out. Louie. "She was fired by the Freezing Works for cruelty to animals."

"She was thrown out of the Iraqi army for brutality."

The lights came up. They were in men's tailcoats and large coloured cravats. Louie's was purple, the other girl's orange. Louie stepped forward first.

"Welcome to the first performance of the soon to be world-

16

famous Comedy Club. You each have a ticket in your hand. I'm going to ask you to do something very important. Tear it up. Go on, tear it up, and throw it away!"

All around Willa people began tearing their ticket and throwing it into the air.

"Good on you. Now say after me. We are all individuals. Go on—we are all—"

Some of the audience began saying it before they realised what they were doing, then they laughed.

"Okay, just a little joke there for the third formers. Now that ticket you just tore up and threw away, that was your politically correct card. From now on you don't have to worry about it. Politics is a four-letter word in the Comedy Club vocabulary. Four letters is as much as Mo can spell anyway, but if you're hooked on being politically correct you might want to leave now. Be a geek now or forever hold your peace!" Nobody moved.

"What we want to know in the Comedy Club, is who first stuck their dirty great political boot into comedians? Humour is universal, right? It's politics that causes all the trouble. If laughter was really the international currency, we'd have no—"

"Mogadishu!" exclaimed Mo.

"Bless you," replied Louie, and the audience laughed.

"Croats, and Kurds!"

"A fabulous vegetarian dish, a traditional staple in the Middle East and Europe."

"Rwanda!" cried Mo, in desperation.

Louie took off flitting around the stage singing, "The Famous Flying Fairy," in a falsetto.

"Gaza Strip," accused Mo, hands on hips.

Music to "Hey Big Spender" came over the sound system and Louie wriggled her body at the audience. "What a nightclub!"

"I mean it, everything is funny, isn't it? How many good jokes have our generation lost to political correctness? Like the one about the Irish abortion clinic—you know, the one that had a nine-month waiting list?"

The crowd laughed, and Louie continued. "We want to reclaim those jokes, reclaim the days when humour was innocent and we could say the word cripple—woops, did I say that?" She put a hand over her mouth. "I really meant physically challenged, of course. Like Mr. Wallis is follicly challenged, and Mrs. Lamont is, well, comically challenged.

"I hate all this political correctness. Don't you? It's so phony. I mean, since when, to get into a government department did you have to be a black, crippled lesbian? Woops! I should say, a physically challenged, alternatively sexually oriented, woman of colour?

"And what's wrong with a few Irish jokes, or Catholic jokes, or Jewish jokes for that matter? What is it about Jewish jokes that so gets up their noses? Oops—did I say noses?"

It went on like that for a while, and the audience laughed more and more at Louie's jokes, often spluttering at how awful they were. Willa smiled at first, but she started to go cold after a while. She wished she hadn't torn up her politically correct card. Then she was angry with Louie. Didn't she see that it wasn't going back to a more innocent time—it was going back to a more bigoted time? Didn't she see that Kevin used exactly the same jokes at Burger Giant, only they were against blondes, or women with big boobs, or just women in general? Willa shuffled her feet as Louie went on about how "Confucius say, No such thing as rape—woman with skirt up run faster than man with trousers down." It was unbelievable that the audience were all laughing at that. Even Geena was howling. It stank. She'd liked Louie, but now she thought she was a real jerk.

Willa stood up and started to move out of her row. Louie was talking about Africa now, and saying something about how their stomachs looked pretty big to her. Geena looked surprised she was leaving so Willa gave her a little wave and kept going. To get to the exit she had to pass right in front of Louie, who was saying, "What's the worst selling book in the history of the world? Huh?" Halfway through it, she caught Willa's eye. Louie faltered in her words for a second, then continued. "The Rwandan cookbook!" Willa didn't smile. She had the feeling eyes were still on her however, and as she closed the door, she saw Louie glancing that way. Tough.

Willa shoved her hands in her pockets and stomped back to her form room. In one pocket she felt a piece of paper. Blue paper. *Die, bitch.* She screwed it up violently and fired it into a rubbish bin.

It was only fifteen minutes later that Willa noticed girls returning to the form room who had been at the Comedy Club. But they were talking quietly and intensely, and looked very serious, nothing like the audience she had left. She was puzzled, and although she tried to keep working on her maths equations, she was keeping an eye out for Geena.

Eventually she arrived, and made a beeline for Willa.

"You missed it. You missed the most amazing thing, Willa."

"What?"

Behind her a group of girls followed. "You walked out, didn't you?" asked one of them, Vika.

"Yeah, I did," replied Willa, cautiously. She didn't want to get into an argument about it.

"Wow. I didn't even think about it."

"It was spooky," said another.

"What? *What?*" Willa demanded of Geena.

Geena sat down on a chair. "Not long after you left, Louie Angelo got really carried away, and the jokes started getting worse and worse. And just when everyone began to feel uncomfortable about them—"

"I was still laughing!" admitted one of the others.

19

"—these pictures started rolling on the big screen behind her. Really ugly things like the bodies of dead Jews at Auschwitz and stuff, and soldiers ransacking villages in Africa. It was gross."

"And then," jumped in Vika, "there was this awful silence, like not a word, except for Louie saying 'A joke's a joke, right?' and this soundtrack started up, of us laughing. It was us, they must have been taping us laughing at Louie before, and it was revolting, these pictures and the sound of all our laughter. There was film of child prostitutes in Asia and all these mental patients left behind in war zones. I thought I was going to be sick."

"It was brilliant," said Geena, simply. "Just brilliant."

Willa smiled down at her page. The maths equations smiled back.

It was after school before she saw Louie again. Willa was in the library looking for some information on John McKenzie for her New Zealand history assignment. It was confusing changing schools halfway through the year—some topics she'd missed altogether, while others she was doing for the second time. And since she was repeating most of her sixth form subjects, there were some, like those in New Zealand Studies, that she was on for the third time. Ms. Rosen had given her a separate assignment to do, and to her surprise, Willa was enjoying it.

Louie came in with Mo and another prefect called Julie. Willa didn't know why, but she watched Louie out of the corner of her eye, and wasn't surprised to see her slip away from the others almost immediately.

"Hi."

Willa looked up and feigned surprise. "Oh, hi."

"That looks heavy," Louie pointed to the *History of New Zealand* Willa had picked out. "What's it for?"

"History. John McKenzie and the breaking up of the Great Estates."

"Uhuh. Umm, Willa, I know you were at the performance at lunchtime—" she began.

Willa didn't help her out. It was cruel, letting her do this, but she wanted to hear what Louie would say.

"I noticed you walked out. Before the end."

"The jokes stank."

"Yeah, they were meant to!" she exclaimed. Louie grabbed a chair and sat beside Willa at the library table. "I mean, that wasn't for real. It was like an experiment, you know, about the politics of humour. To get everyone laughing at awful stuff, and then we turned it on them. We had this film footage of concentration camps and child prostitutes—"

"And soldiers in Africa? Mental patients?" Willa decided to put her out of her misery.

"Yeah!" Louie's face changed. "You knew."

Willa looked at her. "So you just want to make sure I know that you're not an ignorant bigot like everyone else who laughed at the jokes, eh."

Louie's face flushed. She was wearing a loose-necked sweater and Willa watched the pink spread up her neck and ears, against her dark hairline until her cheekbones were fiery red. It gave Willa a fright.

"I'm sorry. It was great what you did." In horror Willa felt her own face begin to heat up. "But really, I could hardly have missed it. It was all anyone talked about all afternoon."

Louie shrugged. "Well, anyway." She picked at something invisible on the table. "For what it's worth, I thought it was great that you had the guts to walk out. You were the only one."

Willa squeezed the edge of the history book and ran the pages between her thumb and forefinger. It made a squirty, fluttery noise.

"I better let you get back to your history," Louie said, pushing back her chair.

"Did you know Ms. Rosen is Jewish?" Willa asked her. Louie stopped, startled. "She was in the audience, apparently. We spent nearly all history period talking about it."

"Really?"

"Uhuh. She said that's what theatre is all about. Challenging ourselves, scaring us." Willa smiled. "You've got another fan, I reckon."

Louie made some really odd movements then and scratched her ankle or something. Willa could only see the back of her curly head and shoulders. Then she stood up abruptly, and looked all around Willa.

"Are you on tonight? At work?" she asked.

Willa shook her head. "Na, I've got fencing on Monday nights."

Louie shuffled a bit longer then said, "Well, I'll see you then," and smiled quickly at the chair beside Willa. And she left.

Willa stared at the *History of New Zealand* blindly. She likes me, she thought. She likes me. And something grabbed in her stomach.

# louie

She didn't even know her last name. Willa. Willa who? And was she a sixth former or a seventh? She'd said she was repeating mostly sixth form subjects, but if she was a sixth, she should be wearing uniform like the rest. Willa had been wearing purple jeans, a long green jersey that fell almost to her knees and a coloured scarf tied into her hair. Louie had felt scruffy and unimaginative in a sweatshirt and plain blue Levis. She didn't usually worry about clothes, but Willa had looked so chic. Louie thought about winding a scarf through her black woolly hair then laughed out loud at the image.

She pushed her bike further up the hill. Even a mountain bike had difficulty getting up Fulton Road, but the rest of the valley was flat for biking to school and it was a rush coming down. This morning, thinking of Willa's comment about speed, Louie had flown down without brakes.

What was it Willa went to on Monday nights—fencing? Louie guessed Willa wasn't the type to spend her spare time stringing number eight wire along farm posts, which meant it must be the other type of fencing. Swords and things. Weren't they on horses? It seemed very romantic and medieval. *Whoso pulleth out this sword from this stone and anvil is the true-born king of all Britain.*

Somehow Louie had the feeling that Willa wouldn't be a royalist either. It was intriguing.

There was something else Willa had said to Louie that stayed in her mind. Something that she was saving up for when she got to the top of the hill. Louie strode faster, pumping her legs and leaning heavily on the handlebars. The top of the rise was a favourite place, where the road bent towards the new housing. Before that bend you could look down across the dark gully of bush to the hills on the far side. When it was quiet and Louie's breathing eased, she could hear the birdsong rise from the bush and float up to where she stood. There was mist hanging about the bush, and despite the occasional flutter of wings it seemed still and primeval. The furthest away hills had a purplish look today, their edges fading in the pale winter light. Louie sucked in the frosty air and felt it caustic in her throat and lungs, then blew out a slow funnel of white breath.

"You've got another fan I reckon," Willa had said. *Another* fan. Did that mean that Willa was the first? Louie let a smile spread on her lips as the call of a tui pierced the air and everything— the bush, the gully, the hills, the blue dome of the sky—seemed to stand still.

Antonio Angelo ran a travel agency in town, imaginatively named Angelo Travel. In business dealings its owner was known as Tony, a man's man who drove a hard bargain, a fair dinkum Kiwi despite his rather poofy surname; when dealing with women or exhorting the beauty of Europe he became Antonio, complete with hand gestures and the edge of an Italian accent. This combined effect made Angelo's the most popular travel agency in town for people who liked to talk with intelligent cosmopolitan men and get a good deal at the end of the day. Louie often met her father in town at the agency and watched him in action, greeting people at the door and ushering them to a seat with his impeccable manners, then telling them how terribly sorry he was not to be able to attend to them personally today, but that his marvellously capable right hand woman would look after them admirably, and of course he would ensure they got the very best package going and how is your delightful daughter Mrs. Dennison he saw her in *La Boheme* and he could honestly say that he had never seen Mimi played with such feeling, what a voice and how proud they must be.

In fact, Tony Angelo had been born and bred in New Zealand and never visited Italy until he was twenty-eight. But his love for his parents' homeland was genuine and he and his wife Susi had made numerous trips back since that first one. Susi, like Tony, was from Invercargill, and was determined to show the world, or at least Dunedin, that Invercargill girls could be as cultured and cosmopolitan as any. The Angelos' house in Garden Village was a statement in architecture, a corrugated iron and glass masterpiece designed for them by a prominent architect, and decorated by Susi according to all the latest trends, complete with stainless steel kitchen and exposed plumbing. This feat didn't mark an end to the interior decorating magazines scattered through the house however. Susi lived in fear of deconstruction going out of fashion.

Louie liked the new house, which she nicknamed the Metal Petal because of the rounded shape of the corrugated iron design. But she missed her childhood home with its well—walls. The new house was so open, with the living areas divided only by wide steel pillars, and huge windows capturing the view across the valley. Susi talked a lot about the house's flow—it has extraordinary flow, she'd say—but Louie felt like she might flow right out the window one day and her mother would simply glance up from her magazine and say, "Look at that. What flow." To combat this irrational fear Louie would move around the house following her outstretched arm like a sleepwalking ballerina saying, "I'm flowing, I'm flowing, I can't stop . . ."

Louie left her bike in the garage and headed for the kitchen. She found a bag of nacho chips and dip in the fridge and settled down in front of the telly. Since Nic had left home it was much quieter round the place, but Louie could hear Marietta playing upstairs on her computer. She grinned. Her mother adored Italian names. Nic had been named after Tony's father Niccolo, she had been named after his grandmother Luisa, but Susi had really gone overboard with her youngest daughter. Marietta loathed her name so much that she had gone for days at a time not answering her family if they used it. She'd been Mary for a while, but hated that now; then she was Marie, but that didn't last a year; now she was insisting that everyone call her Ettie, which Susi refused to do. Marietta had gone off to sulk over the computer for most of the weekend, and Louie guessed she was still punishing them.

Marietta stayed up there until Susi came home and began making the dinner. Then hunger drove her down and as usual an argument about her name followed. When Tony arrived he quietened it down, but it erupted again over the meal and in the midst of the wailing and shouting Marietta knocked over an open bottle of Chardonnay and it broke on the tiles. Louie made her move.

"Dad," she said in her quiet, older and reasonable daughter voice, "I've got to go to work. Could I borrow your car? I think it might rain."

Tony had a second's hesitation before Marietta started up again about her rights as an individual and then he reached into his suit pocket and drew out the keys. This he could deal with. He raised a cautionary finger at Louie. "Nowhere else, and don't speed."

Louie smiled reassuringly and popped the keys in her own pocket. Then she stood up and put a hand on Marietta's shoulder. "You know, arguing while the argu-ee is cleaning up your mess is not very smart," she murmured.

Marietta looked in surprise to where her mother was picking up the shards of glass from under the table, and took her sister's advice. As she left the room, Louie heard her mother say, "Never mind, the tiles needed a good clean anyway."

It was always quiet on a Monday night and Louie and Joan chatted while they packed the few orders and pretended to wipe the cupboards Kevin had told them to clean. Simone was on the counter and another new kid was clearing the tables.

Joan was like the camp mum of Burger Giant. She wasn't super-efficient and sharp-tongued like Deirdre, but she got the work done quickly and laughed at just about anything you said. Louie loved to entertain her and they cackled so loudly a couple of times that Simone poked her head around the divider and told them to shut up. Kevin hung about for a while and tried to get them to come for a drink at his place after work, but Louie thought of Willa and grinned broadly. "Are you serving chicken nibbles?" she said, and after he disappeared Joan doubled up and laughed so hard she had to rush cross-legged to the loo. About ten o'clock Kevin came back in and told Louie in his best managerial voice that she could get away now if she wanted. Louie knew that would mean she didn't get paid for the last half hour, and Kevin was only doing it to get back at her, but she smiled and thanked him all the same.

It hadn't rained. In fact, the stars were sparkling so much in the frosty air that they really did appear to be jumping about in the sky. Louie cruised down George Street in her father's smooth car, listening to the stereo and playing with the electric windows. As she approached the Duke, she slowed and looked inside. There were people in the front bars and lights behind the long-toothed windows upstairs as well.

Impulsively, Louie pulled the car over and parked. A part of her was surprised, and another part was enjoying her own surprise. She was still wondering what on earth to say as she pushed open the door to the public bar.

There had been a rugby match that day, and the room was full of ecstatic rugby supporters. They *had* been ecstatic, rather— now they were drunk, bored and maudlin. Dreadful, mournful singing erupted every few minutes, which usually descended into the famous dreary "Otaaaaa-goh, Otaaaaa-goh," cry of the Otago rugby supporter.

Louie was rather overwhelmed by the smoke, the smell of beer and the number of men in the room, but she weaved her way around groups until she reached the bar. There was a big red-faced man with a completely bald head serving someone, and a collection of men sitting around on stools. Her mother would have described them as "under the weather." A couple of them noticed Louie and seemed to brighten up.

"What have we got here, eh? Gidday love, have a seat," slurred the guy closest to her.

"Oh, Jeez, here we go!" laughed one of his mates.

The first one leaned over to her. He was in his twenties and had wavy brown hair and his lips looked wet. "Don't take any notice of him. Here, honestly, have a stool." He pushed a spare wooden stool behind her so that Louie sort of fell onto it. "I'm Jason," he said, and put out his hand.

"Umm, Louie," she answered and took his hand because she didn't know what else to do. The barman hadn't noticed her yet.

"Louie?" he asked, still holding her hand in his own warm, soft one.

She nodded. There was a lot of noise. "Louie," she said, louder, "As in the kings of France? No? Okay, how about short for Louise?" and then she felt annoyed with herself because she had given him something private.

"Louise," he repeated, nodding in reply. "That's a nice name, it's a lovely name. Now, Louise, can I get you a drink?" he asked, moving his stool closer to her own. He still held her hand and she wished he'd let it go. His friends were groaning and calling out, but he ignored them and fixed his heavy eyes on Louie.

"No—thanks," she added, leaning away from his beery breath, and finally extracting her hand. "I'm just visiting someone."

Just then the bald man from behind the bar came over and said, arms folded on his chest, "I.D?"

Louie paused in confusion and before she could answer, the men around the bar began yelling and booing. "Oh, come on, Sid! She's all right!"

"Best looking thing in the bar all night for godsake!"

"Leave her alone you big bully! You're just too old to remember, you bloody geriatric."

Sid smiled wryly and looked back at her. "Come on, kid, you're too young for here."

This was met with more cat calls and carrying on. Louie tried to say, "I just wanted to see Willa," but nobody heard her and then Jason took her arm and tried to lead her away.

"Come on, it's all right, we'll sort it out. You just sit down here at a table and I'll get you a drink." He pulled a chair out for her and Louie took hold of the back of it but didn't sit down. "She's my daughter!" Jason yelled out to Sid, and the whole place erupted into laughter and banter again.

Sid pointed at her from behind the bar and called, "Out!" very firmly. Suddenly Louie decided that was exactly what she wanted to do, and she turned and headed straight for the door. She had to push her way through a group of men laughing around the entrance. None of them moved for her. As the door closed behind, she heard an aggrieved voice yell, "Ohh, ref!!" and another roar of laughter.

Louie took a couple of breaths of the night air, and savoured the relative quiet outside. Then she walked quickly away from the bar door in case Jason came out following her. She glanced at her father's car, but didn't go to it. Instead, she investigated around the corner of the pub, where she saw a corrugated iron fence and a wooden gate. As she waited for her eyes to adjust there was an explosion of ferocious barking and Judas appeared, paws on the top of the gate, his head snapping at her.

"Judas, Judas, it's all right," Louie tried to calm him, and herself, down. "You know me, remember? I smell good, yeah, sure I do."

He did quieten down a bit, but ruffed a couple more times, and he wouldn't let Louie touch him or come inside the gate. Above, Louie heard a window slide open heavily.

"Judas!" It was Willa. She looked down and there was a pause as she realised who was there. "Louie," she said finally, "—hey."

"Hey." Louie stood and stared at the black figure of Willa outlined against the bright window. "I, um, I was just cruising in the car, you know, getting RSI from electric windows overdose and I remembered you're a night freak too. I figured you'd still be up."

"Logarithms. I've done two in an hour," she replied. "You want some company on your cruising?"

Louie's heart stopped thumping quite so much, and she grinned. "Can your logarithms spare you?"

"Can a bird fly?" She disappeared without waiting for an answer.

Louie patted Judas who was trying to make friends with her again. "A fly can't bird but a bird can fly," she sang softly, and he cocked his head to one side.

Louie had forgotten all Tony's instructions about the car—or if she hadn't altogether forgotten, they just didn't figure suddenly. Was she imagining it, or did Willa seem to know ahead of time what Louie was going to ask? Perhaps it was fate. Louie smiled to herself and opened the gate as Willa appeared out of a lower storey door. Judas acted as if a gigantic bone had just walked into the yard. He whined in excitement and leapt about, his front legs splayed playfully.

"We'll have to take Judas, he'll make a fuss if I leave him," Willa explained.

"Sure." Louie tried not to think what Tony would say about that.

As his mistress approached the gate, Judas rushed in front and tripped her up. Louie grabbed Willa to steady her, only for a second, and it was only on the arm. But it was like a great yell in her head. Willa was wearing a woollen jersey, and it was heavy and warm to touch. Louie let go and rushed to the car where she fumbled with the doors. She felt stupid again, like this after-noon in the library, and her hands still tingled with rough wool.

"Dipstick, Judas," Willa was grumbling at him. "Why d'you always have to go first, huh?"

Willa loved Tony's flash car. "Oh, it's beautiful," she said, running her hand along the leather seat. "What's the engine?"

"Engine?" Louie shrugged, changed gears jerkily and followed the road north, her heart still scudding. From behind Judas pant-ed happily in her ear. He had terrible breath and was fogging up the windscreen. "I wouldn't have a clue." She looked at Willa in the passenger seat. "Would you?"

Willa smiled in reply and turned on the demister. "A bit." Louie watched her hands on the dashboard. Willa had very small, fine hands with milky fingernails, and on her right ring finger she wore a plain gold band. Louie wanted to ask her about it.

"How come? Engines, I mean," said Louie, wondering sud-denly if Willa had a boyfriend.

"My father taught me. He's dead," she said, looking at Louie briefly. "He used to be a truckie. He drove them, and he raced them, and he didn't have any sons. So I spent half my childhood under the chassis of the *Buffalo*. That was his home town," she explained. "Buffalo, New York."

The car headed up Opoho Road almost by itself. Louie had no idea where she was heading. "American?"

"Even liked apple pie, and cried at the anthem. He left when he was a teenager. Came to the big time in Dunedin instead."

Willa laughed and shrugged. "He was a hippie. And he met Jolene."

The road narrowed and veered steeply uphill, leaving the suburban houses behind. It was perfect. Louie swung the car round a bend to the right and felt the tyres grip beneath her. Everything ahead was blackness and bush.

Willa opened her window and tucked her legs up onto the seat. The air blew in the cool, deep smells of the native forest. "Faster," she said quietly, almost as if to herself. Louie paused for a moment then put her foot down and something wild shot through her limbs. The engine surged and gravel spat out to each side of the car. They both leaned to the left and right as the car swung up the winding road, its high beam lighting up the bush ahead.

As they rounded the final corner they saw the road widened into a circle of grass and a carpark, and to the right rose the dark shape of a monument. Louie put on the brakes and some loose stones clattered under the car.

Beyond the monument were the lights of the city. Everything else was black. As Louie opened her door, it swung beyond her hand with the force of the wind on the hilltop. She got out and was knocked a pace backwards—"Wo!"—then she grabbed the car door and heaved it shut again. Willa let Judas out from the back and he leapt away into the darkness.

The monument was a big rectangular shape with what looked like a flagpole on top, but there was no flag. On either side sat giant carved figures of pioneers—one male, one female, wrapped in stone robes and sitting cross-legged like Scottish Buddhas. Louie and Willa felt their way along the railings to the front of the monument. Ahead of them was the fabulous view of the city. The harbour was a black space in the middle, and all around it the yellow, white and red lights spread out over the hills like a huge embroidered coverlet. Above, the stars seemed incredibly close, crushed glass flung across the sky. The wind was freezing and roared in Louie's ears. She opened her mouth wide and gasped into it. Across from her she could just make out Willa's hair whipping about, and watched her raise a pale hand to hold it.

Louie found some steps leading below the monument to a gravel path and bushes. "Here!" she yelled at Willa. "Come down here, it's more sheltered."

There was a rustle in the shrubs beside her and Louie jumped. Judas appeared, his eyes yellow spots momentarily in the blackness, then his breath warm by her hand. Willa was stumbling down the steps.

"God!" she shouted, a bit too loudly for amongst the bushes, "it's freezing!"

Just then there was another movement in the undergrowth and something white zig-zagged ahead of them. A rabbit. Judas's paws skidded on the gravel as he took off after the animal and both plunged into the bush.

"Judas!" yelled Willa, "No! Judas!!" She turned to Louie. "Damn. He thinks he's a great rabbit hunter."

"Can't trust a Judas," Louie replied, flinging herself after him. "Thirty pieces of silver and all that. He's probably dobbing us in. Come on."

She ran ahead, not realising Willa had stopped. Then, turning back, Louie saw Willa stumbling after, her hands and face pale against the bush. "Hang on!" Willa grabbed Louie's arm. "I can't see a thing," she explained.

Louie laughed back, the wind making her feel crazy. She took Willa's hand, and this time it felt good, that small white hand in her own, and they staggered after Judas through the scrub until they reached an open bank of grass that whirred in the wind. Louie spread out her free arm and pulled Willa into a run, and they whooped and laughed, their clothes cracking behind them, until eventually, deliberately really, they fell over in the tussock.

For a while they lay and caught their breath, and let the wind wash over them. In the grass it was much warmer and seemed quiet.

"Dare truth or promise," said Willa suddenly.

"What?"

"Dare truth or promise. You know."

Louie knew. "Truth," she answered, looking up into the blackness.

"Do you believe in God?"

"I guess so."

"You guess so." Willa's tone was flat.

"Don't you?"

"No."

Louie sat up on her elbows and looked at the city lights, the huge audience of the hills. "*The world is charged with the grandeur of God.* Don't you feel it, like electricity? Like now?"

"That's God?"

She laughed and lay back down. "I don't know. My turn. Dare truth or promise."

"Truth."

"Do you have a boyfriend?"

There was a slight shift beside her. "No."

Louie smiled at the sky. "Whose is the ring?"

"That's two questions. Dare truth or promise."

"Truth."

"Don't you ever choose dare?" said Willa. "Okay, have you ever been in love?"

"Since I was about twelve years old with someone or other." Louie heard her words and felt silly.

"Yeah," said Willa.

"Dare truth or promise."

"Dare!"

Louie laughed. "Okay. Stand up and take off all your clothes."

"Get off."

"What can I dare you to do?"

"Just sitting up is hard enough." Willa brushed the hair whipping across her face.

They both sat up, buffeted by the slapping wind. Louie's ears burned but when she put up a hand to touch one it was icy.

"Isn't it stunning?" Willa said, admiring the view.

"My ears are freezing," said Louie. "Feel them!" She grabbed Willa's hand and held it to her right ear. It remained there, even though Louie dropped her own and listened to the faraway sound formed inside the cup of Willa's hand. Her father used to tell her it was the sea. She tried to see Willa's face in the dark but could only make out a pale outline, not her expression. Willa's hand stayed there, surely longer than was normal, still longer again. Her palm was warm against Louie's cheek. *It's happening* she thought, *she's going to do it.* Her throat tightened and a frantic fizzing rose inside her chest. Willa's hand moved slightly, brushing Louie's neck, then she drew it away. Louie choked silently *Don't,* she wanted to say. *Don't stop.*

Instead, she turned back to the view and tried to think of something, anything to say. She was conscious of Willa leaning back on her elbows beside her, quiet. After a bit, Willa jumped up and began walking around, calling out to Judas. Louie swore softly, then got up and joined her.

Judas returned eventually, and hopped happily into the back of the car. It was warm in there, and terribly quiet after the wind, but neither of them spoke. Louie drove carefully down the road this time, wanting the drive to last, wanting to have said something by the time they got back, but the more she tried, the more locked she seemed to be. Willa turned on the stereo and looked out the window. Louie's thoughts became more and more manic. *Say something!* she screamed inwardly, but there it was; not a quote even, a line of Shakespeare, a silly joke within range. Louie Angelo, known as Motormouth to friends and family, every report reminding her that she would do better with a little more attention in class, now, when it felt as if her life depended on it, she simply could not speak. Had she imagined it? Had anything happened at all? Yes. Something had happened, the silence in the car told her that.

When she drew up outside the Duke it was twenty past twelve. Willa leapt out as soon as the car stopped and released Judas. She smiled quickly and unconvincingly. "Thanks," she said in a strained voice. "See ya."

Louie opened her mouth but the noise that eventually came out sounded like a bagpipe—and anyway, Willa had gone.

# willa

She'd had four notes in the last week. All of them were the same; typed, on a slip of plain paper, in a light blue envelope. The envelope was post marked "Dunedin." The first one said, *You're sick*, the second one said, *I know where you are*, the third, *Die, bitch.* The last one, which had arrived today, Willa held in her hands. Its message had thrown her most of all *I miss you*

She breathed in and out shakily. Then she looked at her watch. It was four-thirty, Thursday. She was probably alone at home, like Willa. She picked up the telephone receiver and dialled a number. Then she put it down, and laid her head in her hands. A minute or two later, she tried again. This time she waited.

"Hello? Hello? Are you there?"

"It's me," Willa croaked.

There was a pause, and Willa pressed a palm against her forehead.

"What do you want?" came the voice, tight.

"Cathy, I—I dunno. I just—I thought you might want to hear from me."

There was a snort. "No. I don't." But she didn't hang up.

Willa waited for a little. Then, as she expected, Cathy spoke again. "What you did was wrong, Willa. It was wrong. I'm trying to forget it."

Willa closed her eyes. "We both did it," she said quietly.

There was a gasp from the other end. "I didn't understand what was happening. You know that."

"I've been getting these notes," Willa tried.

"What?"

"Notes. About us. Are they from you?"

"No."

"I thought they might be. I wondered if you were okay. I mean—" Willa held the slip of paper in front of her and stared at it as if it might answer her.

"I don't know anything about any notes. I have to go. Someone could come home."

"The last one said *I miss you*."

There was another long pause. This time it was Willa who broke it. "How are you?" she asked. "Are you all right?"

Cathy's voice was cold. "I'm getting better all the time, now you're gone. My parents and Keith and what friends I have left are very supportive. All I want is for you to stay away from me. For good. Okay?"

Willa screwed up the note in her hand. "Okay," she said, and hung up.

She hadn't talked to Louie for three days. She'd seen her though; running a netball practice, laughing with Ms. Rosen in the foyer, sitting in the prefects' seats at senior assembly. She saw Louie searching for her in the library, but Willa had ducked behind a display screen to hide. Wednesday lunchtime Willa had sat on a bench among the trees outside the prefects' room and watched Louie eat a filled roll and talk with her mouth full. She realised there was definitely something to worry about when that didn't put her off. It took a wood pigeon pooping on Willa's shoulder to drive her inside. Things were looking bad.

Willa didn't know what she wanted. She'd planned to get as quietly as possible through her professional cooking course at this new school, then do a chef's course at Polytech. But there was Louie. It felt as if she'd come from nowhere, exploded from outer space into Willa's life. It was worse than with Cathy. She'd promised herself if she felt like that again, she'd just ignore it. But it wasn't the same. It was worse, it was better, it was stronger. "I didn't understand what was happening," rang Cathy's words in her head.

Willa got changed for work and threw on a jacket. As soon as she touched Judas's lead he whined and tore down the stairs in advance. He seemed to be genetically tuned to notice the slightest scrape of car keys on the bench, the picking up of a jacket or a hand movement within half a metre of the hook his lead hung on. Willa followed him thoughtfully outside, and the walk into town was quiet and cold. Great grey brown clouds hung about the hills, and the sun had already disappeared from Woodhaugh Valley. Some patches of the footpath were still icy from the morning, and Willa's feet crunched on the frost. Even Judas seemed affected by the weather and he walked soberly at her side, with occasional glances up at his mistress.

Louie was already at Burger Giant, and she looked up anxiously when Willa came in the door. Willa recognised the look, and squirmed.

"Hi," she said.

"Howdy!" answered Louie, cheerfully. She came over to Willa holding a huge pile of trays and rubbish. "Welcome to feeding time. Most of the animals are yet to come, but we've done the elephants," she said, nodding towards a table where an obese family of Mum, Dad and three kids squashed into plastic chairs.

Willa laughed, despite herself. Louie followed her into the kitchen and continued. "The monkeys have just arrived," she said, indicating a group of young teenage girls who giggled incessantly, "and boy are they excited about their one trip outside their cages for the day, and yes, here they are, the gorillas!" Five guys in rugby jerseys sauntered in and began joking about how many Giant Burgers they could eat at one sitting. One of the teeny-bopper girls fell off her chair, and the others screamed with laughter. "Oh my," continued Louie, as Willa put on her apron and said hello to Deirdre and Kelly, "we sure are in for a treat tonight. The monkeys are going to do all their tricks to get the attention of the gorillas. What fun!"

Willa joined Deirdre on filling the gorillas' orders (nine Giant Burgers, six large chips, four thickshakes and a large Coke), while Louie washed out her cloths and collected boxes of serviettes for the service bins.

"Deirdre's a real joy germ tonight," she said to Willa when they were sent out to get more trays of buns. "She told Kevin yesterday to order more tomatoes, and he, superbrain, forgot, what else is new, so Deirdre let fly and told him he was bloody useless and if he spent as much time doing the ordering as he does flirting with the staff he'd be halfway competent, so Kevin took her away and apparently gave her a verbal warning. She's spitting, because some friend of hers told her he reckoned Kevin was paid close to forty grand for that piddly little job. And when she told everyone that, Kelly said she thought having all that responsibility he deserved to be paid forty grand, then she was all over him in her break, grovel grovel grovel . . ."

While Louie talked Willa had piled up two stacks of bun trays and handed one to Louie, then picked up the other stack herself. She stood and waited for Louie to take hers back out the door. Louie kept talking furiously.

"You know Kevin used to go out with Kelly—well when I say

go out, he had a one-night stand is as much as we can work out. Kelly talks about their 'relationship' but their dating all seems to revolve around one 'beautiful night in April' when he took her to the wine bar then banged her up at his place. Or that's her story. I wouldn't be surprised if it happened right here. Can't you just see it? Kelly's romantic moment shoved up against the chip warmer? 'Like a piece of breast would you, Kevin?' 'Is this a drumstick I see before me?' Poor Kelly, I don't think he's even looked at her since. Except for the apron routine of course, you know—"

Willa put her stack of trays down, and Louie stopped. "I didn't know you burbled," Willa said.

She watched as Louie's neck turned pink again, and her voice stuck. Poor Louie, she thought. It's all or nothing words-wise. Willa wanted to tell her it was all right, there was no need to panic.

"Probably he was the first guy Kelly had sex with," she said, instead. "It's understandable, isn't it, that she can't let go? If she admits he's a creep, that makes her the fool you obviously think she is, doesn't it?"

"Well, yeah, I guess," Louie frowned, bright red.

"They need these buns, Louie."

After that, Louie stuck to clearing tables, and Willa to filling orders. She could see Louie was upset, and was keeping a wide berth around Willa. Deirdre was in a foul mood, so there wasn't much chance to talk anyway. It got so busy that Kevin took orders out the front with Simone all night. He was making quite an effort, Willa noticed, keeping serious and professional to prove his point to Deirdre. At eleven o'clock it was a relief for Willa to take off her uniform and leave the tense atmosphere.

She wandered outside to collect Judas. Louie was sitting on a brick wall patting him. She looked up as Willa came over. "Hi."

Willa nodded. She didn't trust her voice suddenly. Maybe she'd say something hard and cold and make Louie go away again.

She didn't want that. Willa untied Judas and let him trot around the loading dock.

"I wanted to say I'm sorry," Louie began. "About, you know — burbling." She smiled hopefully at Willa.

"Hey, Louie, don't be silly," said Willa, and put her hand on Louie's arm instinctively. *Don't touch her!* she screamed at herself, and quickly drew her hand away again. "I was just being smart."

Louie nodded her head around in a way that Willa was starting to recognise as a sign of embarrassed pleasure. "I do it, I know, sometimes. I just don't know how to stop." And she stopped abruptly, as if she was testing herself out.

"Yeah, well, at least you're funny."

"Willa," Louie said, in a soft serious voice, "I wanted to say — since the other night . . ."

Suddenly Willa noticed Louie was trembling. It was cold, but not that cold. *Shit,* she thought. *Shit shit shit. This is too quick.* "I can't talk, Louie. I have to go."

But she couldn't go, not while Louie's eyes held hers like that. "I've missed you."

Willa reeled as if she'd been hit. She saw the note from this afternoon in her hand. It was all happening again. *No.*

"Just drop it, Louie," she said, standing up. "We hardly even know each other." She called Judas, and picked up her bag. Then, without looking at Louie's face, she marched down the alley as fast as she could.

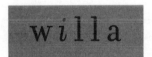

It might have worked with Cathy. Louie was too direct, and too sure of herself. She caught up with Willa walking home after school the next day.

"You're right. We hardly know each other. I've got no right to miss you when you're not around. But there it is. I do."

Willa stared at her. There was no answer to this, only the ecstatic internal battle she knew was not going to go away.

"Dare truth or promise."

"Louie . . ."

"Dare truth or promise."

"Okay. Dare."

"Dare you to teach me fencing."

"Fencing?"

"Isn't that what you do on Monday nights?"

Willa frowned. "Yeah. You want to join?"

"No. I want you to teach me how to fight with swords. For *Twelfth Night*. The play."

"Play?"

"It's the main production this year. Mrs. Ashton has cast me as Viola. She spends most of the play dressed up as a boy, and at one point she gets into a sword fight." Louie shrugged helplessly.

"I've got two left feet, well three when I get confused, and as for my arms, well, they argue amongst themselves and both hate my legs . . . I um, I don't know where to start."

Willa sighed. "I use foils mostly, I've only just started épée. That's a larger, heavier sword, but . . ."

"Perfect. When do we start?"

Even if she'd wanted to, Willa couldn't get out of it. Her defence against Louie's honest charm was woeful. She mentally lowered her shields in defeat. "Okay. Saturday afternoon, I'm in a tournament," she told Louie. "It wouldn't be hands on for you, but you could watch, get the hang of it. Then maybe I could give you a lesson on the basics."

Louie gave her a cheeky grin. "Great! And I'll try not to miss you between now and then."

"Hey, Louie, I don't know why I said that. I overreacted." Willa noticed that despite the bravado, Louie's neck was bright red again. "In fact," Willa said, now giving her horse its head and charging with the enemy, "I missed you too."

The road was already glittery with early frost, and their breaths were like little ghosts. Louie pushed her bike so it tick-ticked beside them. They talked about family. Louie told Willa about Nic who only came home now for washing or food, and about Marietta's name war. She described her father's travel agency, the Metal Petal and her mother's obsession with flow. Willa wondered at such a life. She noticed there was no mention of going to church.

At the back gate of the Duke Judas leapt in greeting and swept Louie's legs for scents. They kept talking. Willa wanted her to stay, but she wanted her to go, too. *Don't make me invite you inside.* Louie stayed, apparently unaware, chatting, joking, playing with Judas, until it began to get gloomy and the air pressed low. There was no escaping it.

"It's cold. Do you want to come in?"

"Thanks." Louie smiled so charmingly that Willa felt like water.

She led Louie through the carton- and crate-lined storeroom, lurid red hall and upstairs. In the kitchen Willa silently emptied the ashtray of pink smudged cigarette butts into the rubbish and switched on the kettle. Only then did she risk a glance at Louie.

She was tickling Elvis's green feathered breast with her forefinger. The budgie mouthed her finger in its beak, then bit her, hard. Louie yelled and told him off. "Nice bird," she said to Willa.

"You'd be cranky too if you were locked in a cage all day."

*"A Robin Red breast in a cage, puts all Heaven in a rage."*

There it was. Heaven again. God.

"Milk?"

"And sugar. Is that your father?" She was looking at the wedding photo on the wall.

"Yep." Willa followed her through to the living room where Louie was looking at the small bookcase of paperbacks. *Go on, say it. What a dump. What a bunch of losers.* But Louie was smiling and pulling out some comics. "Yay, Asterix, my favourite." She looked up at Willa. "What's it like living in a pub?"

It was no use. You couldn't not like Louie. Sprawled in front of the heater, Judas's chin on her leg, Willa explained how in their hippie days her parents had named their two daughters Bliss and Willa and how she had grown up in pubs amidst country and western music. "It was quite an education," she said, watching Louie flick through Jolene's old photo album.

As the long windows turned black they talked about school and their plans—Willa's to be a chef, Louie's to be a lawyer. "Sure got the gift of the gab," Willa laughed, and then thought about the gummed up silence in the car the other night. By the time Louie finally got up to leave, Willa could hardly believe she hadn't wanted to invite her in.

"Hey, this fencing thing," said Louie at the door. "What about the horses? Where do they come from?"

Willa looked at her strangely. "Horses? There aren't any horses." Then she burst out laughing. "What *are* you thinking of? Jousting, polo, perhaps? Hip hip, jolly good show and all that . . ."

"Yeah!" laughed Louie, swinging onto her bike. "For all I know you're Prince Charles's love child. I mean, swords, please? We're talking about a very weird sport here."

"Better not say that in front of the others on Saturday," said Willa, lifting an eyebrow. "There's some psychopath material there if you ever saw it."

# l o *u* i e

Louie watched as Willa walked neatly to the mat. A young man was attaching a wire to her white jacket and Willa pressed her foil delicately against the chest of her opponent to ensure the red light appeared on contact. Both fencers raised their foils to their foreheads, saluting firstly each other and then the judges, and Louie thought of Sir Lancelot saluting Guinevere before spurring his horse and galloping off full tilt, his lance gallantly held horizontal above his shoulder. It was a pity that there were no horses.

They donned their masks — donned being the type of word Louie imagined fencers used all the time — and began to fight. Willa's red ponytail flapped up and down against her shoulder blades like a fox struggling to be free. Their feet swished and occasionally stamped on the mat, and the foils squeaked and slid off each other repeatedly. Willa's opponent, a forty-year-old man, his baldness disguised by the mask, was surprisingly quick and agile, and he heralded each of his serious attacks with a loud series of grunts.

Louie wasn't sure who was scoring the points, although at each hit the fencers stopped and the judges made it clear. Louie wasn't sure because something extraordinary had happened to her. It had become obvious to her that she was sitting in a cold gymnasium that smelt of old socks halfway across town from home, amongst the kookiest group of people she had ever met, watching a sixth form girl have a sword fight with a middle-aged man. The air tightened to a drum skin and all Louie could see were Willa's legs advancing and retreating fast and crab-like, her neat white body moving in purposeful, clean patterns. It was so like Willa, this sport, so right, so singular, so perfectly odd, that Louie felt a strange complete heat well up and fill her from head to toe, and she knew. She knew that there was only one reason she was in this damp smelly gym, she knew that there was only one thing in it that mattered to her, and she knew that it was the one thing that mattered most to her in the whole world.

"I'm in love with that girl," she said out loud in amazement, because she knew that this was a life-changing thing and life-changing things should be said aloud, should have a moment in time, and a place in the air, some molecular structure to make them real. *I'm in love with that girl,* she heard as it reverberated inside her head. And it was a truth, she realised, as things are which you don't think, but discover have always existed.

Just then the bout ended. Willa, the victor, took off her mask with her free hand and turned in one movement to where Louie was in the stand, and raised her foil in salute. Louie was already on her feet, the warmth in her body having overflowed into a standing ovation and a magnificent, startling grin that she bestowed regally on her Lancelot.

Afterwards, Louie watched as Willa was presented with a small silver cup, and everyone cheered. There were about fifteen people there, most of whom were men, and many of them quite old. Two of the women were wives who fenced with or against their husbands. Good way to let off a bit of marital aggression, Louie thought. There were three guys from university—a weird spotty politics student called Lucan, a nice spotty physics student called Marcus and one beautiful blonde theology student with an English accent called Christopher. They all seemed keen on Willa.

When the prize-giving was over, and the others disappeared, Willa went to a carton of gear and pulled out clothing for Louie. The jackets came with inside pockets on the chest for plastic cups which Willa, laughing, called boob-protectors. Louie felt her face flush as Willa chose the right size for her, then helped her put it on. She showed Louie how to stand properly on guard, with her left hand held up like a jug handle behind, how to step forward and back, crablike, and how to "lunge" at your opponent. Louie had a tendency to lunge right down onto the ground in front of her where her crab impersonations were at their finest. Standing, Louie kept dragging her left shoulder round and facing front-on instead of side-on. To overcome this she decided to try fighting two ways at once with a foil in each hand. She became very good at the atavistic grunts and French exclamations, and her Errol Flynn and Basil Rathbone impersonations up the stairs were impressive, especially since she was taking both parts. Then she pulled Willa out of the gear cupboard and apologised for being a hyperactive student. After nearly an hour Willa said she'd got the hang of the basics and that would do for now. She locked up the gym and they went downtown for a coffee.

Neither was working that night. "It's Saturday night and there's nothing happening," moaned Willa, and Louie wondered if she usually went out to parties with the other fencers. She hated not knowing about Willa's other life, the life at the pub, the fencing, what she did on Saturday nights.

"Saturday night? It has no meaning," Louie shrugged. "I'm so used to working, I don't know what to do with it." *Spend it with me.*

"There's one thing we could do," said Willa, scraping out the froth at the bottom of her cappuccino and sucking on the spoon. "But we'd need a car."

Louie smiled. "I am numero uno daughter. Marietta's teacher called Mum and Dad into school yesterday. In comparison with little sister I can do no wrong."

"We-ell . . . dare truth or promise. Choose dare, go on."

"Dare."

"Get the car, and pick me up at seven."

# louie

"A pub? She lives in a pub?" Susi's eyebrows rose above the stainless steel cooktop. "It doesn't sound very nice."

"What does 'nice' mean? There's nothing wrong with it. It's just a live-in job, that's all."

"Her father runs it then, does he?"

Louie leaned on the bench and picked at the grated cheese. "No, her mother does. Her father's dead."

"Dead? Oh, poor kid."

"Well, not recently. He died racing trucks, you know, big rigs and that. Years ago. He was American."

Susi stopped stirring the sauce and looked at Louie for a moment, then resumed. Louie continued talking about Willa, although she was vaguely aware that she was heading towards Burble City.

"Her mother's name's Jolene. She and Willa's dad were country and western singers. Her mum's from Gore, you know," Louie invented, thinking that her Southland mother would approve of that, but Susi's face didn't alter. Louie tried harder.

"They travelled all around the States singing as Buddy and Jo Apple," Louie said, filling in the gaps in Willa's story. "Apple wasn't their real name, that was their singing name. Then they came to Dunedin and had two kids and bought a country and western bar. But Buddy crashed the *Buffalo,* that was his rig, and died. Willa was only eleven years old. She said her mother hardly ever sings now, and she smokes like a train so her voice is probably shot to bits anyway." Louie paused, remembering Susi hated smokers. "Willa doesn't smoke," she added.

Susi was unimpressed. "I should hope not."

"No, she's not what you think, pub and all that. She's really—stylish—she wears amazing clothes, and winds scarves in her hair and stuff. She's much better looking than I am."

"Is she really. Lou," she said, turning the gas down, "if you can take your mind off the wonderful Willa for a moment, grate me some more cheese to make up for what you've eaten, will you."

Louie bit her lip. "It's not the 'wonderful Willa,'" she said, and fossicked in the cupboard for the cheese grater. "She's just an ordinary Willa, as Willas go, although it's not a common name is it . . . I wonder if it's short for something. God, I hope it's not Wilhemina." Susi was staring at her. "Um, what was the question?"

"Here," said her mother, handing her the grater from the bench. "Well, as far as visiting this Willa person goes, you'll have to ask your father. I'm taking my car to Bernadette's for a parish meeting tonight. Surely you can ride your bike that far."

"No, I can't. It's a pain coming back up the hill at night, and it's got a slow puncture," she lied.

Her father also objected to the mention of a pub, despite Louie's insistence that they weren't going to be drinking.

"We're not even going to stay there!" Louie blurted out, then rolled her eyes at her stupidity.

"Where are you going then?" demanded her mother.

"I mean, we might not stay there. We might go—I don't know, Willa had some idea, but she didn't tell me."

"Let's get this straight," said Tony, looking at her levelly. "You want to borrow my car, you don't know where you might be going, you're meeting at a pub and you're going with a girl we haven't met."

"Sounds... the tiniest bit flaky, I'll give you that. But Dad, we're probably going to watch television. Honestly, it's no big deal. If we do anything, it'll just be a drive to somewhere nice, you know, with a view or something."

Tony and Susi looked at her suspiciously.

"A view," repeated Tony.

"Who is he?" Susi folded her arms.

"What?"

"There's a boy in this. Don't try and pretend there isn't, Louie. You've spent an hour and a half trying on clothes and used just about all the mousse in the house. You don't do that when you go out with a girlfriend."

Louie closed her eyes. She didn't know whether to laugh or scream.

She screamed.

"Don't you realise this is the first Saturday night I've had free for God knows how long? Every bloody weekend I'm working. Not to mention just about every free evening. And I still manage somehow to get my homework done, to do every assignment and essay they throw at me. You don't have to drop everything and rush into school to see my teachers. You don't have to stand over me to make sure I study for exams like you did with Nic. All I'm asking is that you trust me. Why can't you do that? There is no boy. We're not planning to do anything stupid. I just wanted to go out tonight and take it as it comes, that's all."

Louie had got the car, along with a lecture about trust. Great, she thought, opening Willa's gate, I'd like to tell them the truth and see how much they trust me then. She hugged her coat closer. She had bought an old suede jacket at an op shop last week, and it was like wearing a saddle. It was warm though, and looked like something she might have thrown on as she went out the door. In fact Louie had tried on absolutely everything she owned to go under it. In the end she'd opted for a dark top and black jeans.

The door opened as she raised her hand. A woman with red hair and a dish of dog food stood there with Judas. Judas immediately barked at Louie, but he was quickly distracted by the food and went back to the woman.

"Hello, a beatnik!" she said. "Calm down, Judas."

Louie almost looked behind her. The woman laughed a deep, throaty chuckle. "You must be here for Willa."

Louie nodded, and tried to pat Judas, but he ducked away from her and followed his dish. The woman placed the bowl on the concrete. Then she turned to Louie.

"I'm Jolene, Willa's mum."

"Louie. Louie Angelo."

"Come in." Jolene, who showed no traces of her country and western background in a mohair jersey and polyester slacks, led Louie to the stairs. Through the glass doors off the hall Louie could see and hear the bar and she hoped none of the rugby guys from the other night could see her.

Willa was in the kitchen upstairs. Jolene walked in first, and announced, "There she is. Sixties," she said, gesturing to Louie, "meet the seventies!" And she shut the door behind her.

Willa was wearing a long, embroidered coat that fell around her ankles, and tooled leather boots. Her hair was loose, with just a brightly-coloured scarf holding it off her face. Louie shook her head, confused.

"What's she on about? Sixties, seventies? And what's a beatnik?"

Willa laughed like her mother and shrugged. "Hey, I love that jacket. And it's perfect for where we're going."

"Which is?" Louie sat down but stood up again immediately. The argument with her parents was gone; she was suddenly excited.

"Now that would be telling. It's a dare, remember?" Willa smiled at her and stood up too. "You drive and I'll navigate, okay?"

"Deal."

It was dark and warm, a strange nor'west wind rippling over the hills, as Louie and Willa motored over the open road south of the city. All around was farmland, and the occasional whiff of sheep or silage made them screw up their faces and buzz the windows shut in a hurry. Louie drove fast to please Willa and smooth round the bends, over rises, down dips. "Hang a right," Willa said at one point, then "left, to the end of the road," then "right, and right again." There were no houses where she'd led Louie. There were no lights, just the vacuous black bucket of the sky punctured by sharp white stars. Finally, Willa directed her down a long gravel road and they parked in what appeared to be a patch of farmland in the middle of nowhere.

"What is this?" Louie shook her head, puzzled. "Are we meeting a UFO or what?"

"Something like that." Willa jumped out of the car. Louie shrugged to herself and followed. To her right she suddenly noticed there were lights—coloured lights.

"Willa, what's . . . ?" They looked familiar. Blue lights, several of them as she looked harder. And further away some red ones and a building. The wind buffeted her off balance for a moment.

"It's the airport," she said out loud, realising. "It's the airport, isn't it, and that—that's the runway!"

Willa was striding away into the black. "Yep. Come on, over here."

"I don't believe this. I do not believe it." Louie broke into a jog and strained her eyes to see where Willa had gone. A few hundred metres across paddocks and over a wire fence, she caught up with her.

"There," Willa said with satisfaction. "There she is."

Louie followed her gaze. They stood about a paddock's length away from the end of the runway, staring straight down the two lines of neon blue spots. At the far end of it were the flashing red and white lights of an airplane coasting into position.

"Oh shit. Oh my god. Is that thing going to take off? It is, isn't it?" Louie looked at Willa, her heart already beginning to pump. "You're mad. You're absolutely bloody crazy. *This* is your idea of fun?"

Willa was transfixed by the sight of the plane. They could hear its engines in the distance—the combination of roar and whine that always thrilled Louie.

"You wait," Willa whispered, and Louie looked at her for a moment, noting the fix of her eyes, the tension around her jaw-line and the little vein pulsing at her temple. *I am out of control,* she thought. *If she asked me to throw myself under a jumbo's wheels I'd say front or back ones?*

The plane had come to a halt, facing them. For the first time Louie saw that planes had white headlights shining from their undercarriage. She felt like a possum caught in their light. "Do you think he can see us?" she whispered. "The pilot, I mean?"

Willa didn't answer. The engines whirred ferociously, and the plane began to move forward. At her side, Willa's hand found Louie's, and they stood, frozen to the spot.

At first it seemed incredibly slow, as if it were just rolling towards them, and Louie could make out people in the flight deck, dimly lit. Then suddenly the lights at the end of each wing flashed violently, wider and wider, and Louie could see for the first time the body of the plane, its bulk bearing down on them, rushing at them, huge wings outstretched. The sound was over-whelming, shrieking at them, blaring. Louie wanted to cover her ears, but she didn't want to let go of Willa's hand. She dug in her nails as the plane ate up the runway, murderous. Just as her legs began to dissolve, the white lights at the front lifted, and a blast of hot air and thunderous noise burst from under the aircraft. It screeched above them, its white body burning through the air and the surrounding blackness wobbling in its heat. The smell of burning rubber and exhaust filled Louie's nostrils and mouth, which was open and screaming now, screaming for all she was worth.

She was jumping too, jumping up, down and around, and then her arms were around Willa, squeezing her, still yelling and whooping, and Willa was yelling back. They leapt about in a circle for a bit before Louie realised that she actually had her arms round Willa, *embracing* her, and she decided not to let go.

To let go would mean to wait until she had this good an excuse again, and she didn't know when that might be. Louie couldn't bear it anymore. *To hell with it,* she thought, *to hell with it.* They stopped jumping and turning, they stopped yelling, and Louie gripped on to Willa, hugged tighter even, and buried her head in her shoulder. Her heart was still thumping, and she could feel Willa's too, like a bird's belting against her ribcage.

Then Willa's arms moved, and Louie caught her breath in fear, terrified she would pull away. She didn't. Her hand cupped Louie's head, ran down the back of her hair, her neck, and lay cool and gentle under her collar. Her other arm moved lightly up her back and rested there. What a difference, the quality of the touch, the subtle shift in placement, that turned a hug into a hold. Louie wanted to cry, to weep with relief. She relaxed her wrestling grip and leaned into Willa, nuzzled her heavy hair, felt the soft skin under her ear, breathed in her smell.

When Willa turned and kissed her, Louie thought in her head, *this is my first kiss.* It wasn't, of course, she'd kissed a number of boys, and done more too, but she'd never, ever felt as if she were falling off a cliff. She'd never before felt as if her body were being turned to water from the inside out, or as if they were both whirling through space into an airless black vortex. Louie felt all these things, and above all, a disbelief, a wild, terrifying disbelief that this should be happening—no, not that she was in love with a girl, for it seemed suddenly absolutely natural that she should be in love with this girl—but that, god only knew how, this girl should love her back!

It was Willa who finally pulled away, who said, looking at the ground, "Do I shock you?"

Louie reached and touched her cheek, frowning and smiling together. "No, Willa. You don't shock me."

Willa turned slightly away and sat on the ground. An icicle slid down Louie's back. *Don't turn away, not now, please.*

She crouched down beside Willa and looked beyond her into the invisible distance. "I didn't think this could happen. This," she said, gesturing like her father, palms upward, "—it just blows me away. I didn't dare believe you might be feeling the same."

"Ohhh," Willa groaned, and swung back to her. "You didn't guess? God, Louie, I haven't been able to think of anything else since the day I met you."

"Really?" Louie was delighted. She touched Willa's arm, her shoulder in its embroidered coat. It was so strange, so new to do that, and Louie felt awkward suddenly, as if she didn't know how.

"Louie," Willa wrapped her arms around her knees and stared back down the empty runway. "There's something I have to tell you." Her voice was strained, choked. She turned to Louie, who was feeling that same icicle slide down her back. "This isn't the first. I've had a . . . a relationship before."

Louie blinked. "With a woman?"

"Her name was Cathy. She was my best friend at Miller Park. It happened in the Christmas holidays." Willa's arm jerked as she pulled at some grass and Louie heard the tuff, tuff of it coming away. "Neither of us were really sure about it. Well, Cathy got pretty weird, and I tried to end it, then she got more upset. I just didn't know what to do, what she wanted me to do. Does this make any sense?"

Louie nodded.

"I really ended it back in February, but every now and then she'd spin out and I'd get a panic call. She was freaked out by her family. They're fundamentalists, and she was terrified her step-father would find out. Also she thought God was going to send her to eternal damnation or something."

Louie snorted a little, then wondered what the Catholic Church's view would be. She had a fair idea.

"One day, a few months ago now," Willa continued, "I got this phone call from her and I went around. She was in a mess and I was just hugging her, you know, not doing anything, and her weird stepbrother came in. Keith. He was always hanging around. Anyway, he went berserk and started all this arm waving and calling down God and so on, and next thing I know all their family are there, and Cathy's taking their side. They called the school, they called my mother, it was hideous."

"Oh, Willa."

She turned to Louie fiercely. "I want you to know this. I want you to know everything, and then if you don't want to have anything to do with me, go now. Go now, Louie, because I can't help what I feel."

This time Louie touched her without awkwardness, she held her close and Willa clung to her. "I'm not afraid, Willa," she said. "I love you, and I'm not afraid of that."

## willa

Judas knew about hats too. As soon as she shoved the black hat on her head he began leaping about and sniffing at the door. Willa ignored him. She looked again at the photo Louie had given her. It was a picture of the two of them in a field, an enormous blurred aeroplane behind them. Louie was crouched, laughing, her hands over her ears, and Willa was jumping high, one arm outstretched, the other out of the picture as if she was being snatched away by someone invisible. They'd been back at the airport several times now, and the last time Louie had brought her super-duper automatic everything camera and set it up on a fence post to take photos of them. Willa carefully put it back in her wallet just as the phone rang.

It was Louie.

"When are you coming?" she asked.

"I was just about to leave."

"Good."

"Why, am I late?"

"No, no." Louie lowered her voice. "I just wanted to hear your voice, that's all. Dad's had another argument with Marietta so she'll be grumpy."

"Oh great."

"It's all right, no one takes any notice of her. Nic's arrived too. Must have smelt the cooking. Anyway, come soon, please."

"I'm on my way."

"Judas?"

"He's coming too. Is that all right?"

"Yep, fine. See you then."

"See you." Willa was smiling to herself.

"Bye.

"Bye.

"Au revoir."

"Louie, this is dumb. I'll be there in ten minutes." Willa hung up and hustled Judas out the door.

Tony Angelo was in expansive mode. He waved his arms in welcome to Willa, he laughed and seemed delighted by the addition of Judas, he even included them both in an unconventional Grace before the meal. Willa smiled politely but sat through it with her eyes open. Marietta glowered at everyone like a squat little volcano. Nic concentrated on eating as much as possible — his foray into student flatting was a severe disappointment in the food stakes, and next year they'd resolved to get some female — preferably Applied Science female — flatmates. He was delighted to hear that Willa was doing professional cookery. Louie was nervous, Willa could tell, and talked in competition with her father, loudly interrupting his stories to correct or admonish him, capping them with funnier ones of her own. Tony popped open bottles of wine in punctuation to their banter. They did a great double act.

It was Susi who worried Willa. She was the perfect hostess, quietly plying everyone with more food and slipping back and forth from the kitchen with dish after dish of culinary delights. Her cooking was fantastic. Busy though she was, Susi's careful eye was at work continually. On several occasions Willa had caught Susi regarding her thoughtfully, and the rest of the time she watched Louie with a mixture of pleasure and concern. As she laughed at Louie's ebullience Susi's eyes would flicker about the table, always stopping at Willa two or three times, and Louie herself couldn't glance at Willa without Susi's immediate scrutiny. *She knows,* Willa thought, *somehow she knows.*

"This is wonderful, Mrs. Angelo," Willa volunteered, tasting the dessert. "What's in it?"

Susi smiled glassily at Willa. "Thank you. It's chocolate and Cointreau, with egg and cream, basically. You have to beat the egg whites separately"

"It's wonderfully fluffy."

"Did you notice it was fluffy, Nic?" Louie asked her brother sweetly.

Nic was already scraping the bottom of his glass with a long spoon. "Hrmphh," he grunted and gave her a withering look. "Is there any more, Mum?" he asked, and when she nodded, he scrambled up first. "No, it's all right, I'll get it, I'll get it." He brought back a bowl to the table and offered it first to Willa, with a warm smile.

Nic was taller than his father but similar in looks, as was Louie. Willa found it strange looking at Nic's dark, curly hair, especially his long-lashed brown eyes and seeing parts of Louie. He was slower than she was though—slower in speech and thought, less frenetic, less interesting.

"No thank you," she said, and Nic helped himself.

"Nic!" cried the others.

"What? What? I offered it to the guest first!"

Louie rolled her eyes. "You're such a charmer."

"*Grazie,* Luisa."

This time she groaned. "Oh god, not the Italian." She turned to Willa. "Nic flunked six months of Italian in the fourth form and has been trading on *grazie* and *prego* ever since."

"It's more than you know, ignoramus."

"I know more than anyone," announced Marietta. *"Buona sera. Io sono Marietta. Ne ho dodici. Quanti anni ha?"* Marietta recited, posing to an invisible audience.

The others clapped sarcastically, Tony crying *"Bravo! Bravissimo!"* Louie looked apologetically at Willa.

"So, Willa," began Tony, and Willa half-choked on a mouthful of Sauvignon. "Gosh, the wine's not that bad is it? Susi—you bought this sav blanc—Willa doesn't like it."

"No, no, I—" Willa exploded into another bout of coughing. "Please..." Then Nic was beside her with a glass of iced water. "Oh, thank you." Her throat cleared, Willa took a deep breath.

"All I was going to ask you," continued Tony, "was whether you spoke any languages, but no, let's not start on that again. What do you think of, let me think, what shall we test her with..."

"Dad," moaned Louie, "don't be horrible."

"I'm not being horrible, I'm just..."

"Testing her. On one question, of your choosing. What a Fascist."

"Fascist?"

"Louie," frowned Susi, "don't be so dramatic."

"No, no, even Nic agrees, I'm a Fascist. My customers think I'm nice, you know," Tony told Willa. "But my children, they think I am a cross between Mussolini and Saddam Hussein. No wonder I spend so much time at work, huh? More wine, Willa? Now," he turned to his children, "is that the question of a Fascist?"

Marietta, surreptitiously trying to steal Susi's glass of wine, smiled sweetly at her father. Louie said "Yes," and Nic said "Not if you fill mine at the same time."

"Now Willa," Tony began again, "I know, I'll ask you about yourself. That's hardly a Fascist approach, is it?"

"Don't even answer him," said Louie.

"What do you want to know?" Willa asked, feeling five sets of Angelo eyes zero in on her.

"Hmm. Well, I think one question each is fair and democratic, isn't it? One question from each member of the Angelo family isn't too much to ask in return for dinner and then we'll . . . mark you out of ten and let you know if you can stay friends with Louie."

"Oh, for god's sake."

"Louie," warned Susi from the kitchen. "Language."

"My question is . . . dogs. Easy. Who would you save from in front of a speeding car—Judas, or me?"

There were groans and replies from all round the table. Willa laughed and said, "Judas." Tony, shocked and delighted, stood up and pretended to order her out of the house. Willa noticed he had very white teeth and smelt of wine, but not unpleasantly so.

"What about me?" asked Marietta, ready to ask her question.

"No," teased Tony, sitting back down, "anyone would save Judas before you. Now, hang on, I'm not finished." Tony held up his hand to the protestations. "What about Judas or Nic? Eh?"

Willa caught Louie rolling her eyes. "Judas," announced Willa again, and Nic tossed his napkin in the air and shrugged.

"Always the same. Nobody cares about poor old Nic."

"You'd save a hedgehog before Nic."

"Okay," Tony's voice carried over the noise, and Willa knew what was coming. "What about Louie, eh? I mean she did invite you here after all, she is meant to be your friend."

"But she doesn't sit when she's told to, and she's expensive to feed," said Nic.

"Look who's talking."

Willa looked at Louie across the table, so uncomfortable, so bristling with mixed messages. "I'd save Louie," she answered.

There was a moment's pause in which the air tingled but Willa didn't care.

Then Marietta piped up. "My turn. Okay, how come you're wearing different earrings?"

Willa smiled. "I couldn't decide which to wear."

"You should have worn the paua ones," Marietta advised.

"My turn." Nic put one hand over Marietta's mouth.

"Yes?" Willa noticed Susi listening carefully as she came in with a tray of coffee.

"Why'd you leave Miller Park School. Were you expelled?"

Tony snorted. "Nic."

But Nic's eyes twinkled. "No love lost now. She didn't save me from the speeding car, remember." He let go the squirming Marietta who leaned forward eagerly to hear the answer.

"This is daft," said Louie, folding her arms. "Mum, tell them to stop."

Susi smiled benignly. "No thank you, Lou. I'm rather enjoying it."

"This is where democracy gets you," Tony taunted his daughter.

"Well?" Nic was enjoying Willa's discomfort. She tried not to look at Louie this time.

"The principal and I agreed to differ, as they say, eh. I fancied a school in the twentieth century."

"Well fielded, well done," clapped Tony. "Spoken like someone heading for a career in the diplomatic service!"

"Louie, your turn," said Susi.

"No thank you."

"Go on, Lou, you're never stuck for something to say."

Louie swung round to her brother. "I prefer to let people tell me what they want when they're ready. That's what people out there in the real world call friendship."

"Ooo, uppity, uppity."

"Willa doesn't have to answer anything she doesn't want to," Susi assured her daughter. "Well, if you don't have a question it's only me left."

Willa waited, and the dessert did a slow, sickly flip in her stomach.

"I know," said Susi brightly. "Tell us about your boyfriend."

Louie's eyes closed and she leaned back in her chair. Willa tried to keep her face utterly expressionless.

"I don't have a boyfriend," she answered as lightly as she could.

"None at the moment," Susi corrected her. Nic leaned his head to one side slowly and regarded Willa. "Well," Susi continued, "tell us about your Ideal Man." She lifted a glass to her lips and grinned at her husband as if she were being innocently provocative.

*We understand each other very well,* thought Willa, keeping her eyes on Susi.

"I don't think I have an Ideal Man, either," she answered very carefully. "I think—I think people just happen, don't they. Love just happens. And then everything is changed, forever." Willa moved her glance to Louie, who sat stock still, her eyes locked onto Willa's.

"Indeed," murmured Susi.

Willa stayed the night. Susi made a big deal of fixing up Louie's spare bed, turning on the electric blanket and putting Judas firmly outside the ranchsliders. Louie fidgeted at her side until she was finished and then closed the bedroom door.

"I wish it had a lock," she said, leaning against it.

They stood in silence for a bit, listening to Susi's movements. Finally they heard her in the bathroom upstairs.

"About time," muttered Louie, coming to her. Kissing Louie still blew Willa's mind. She'd expected it to be like kissing Cathy, but that had always been a physical attraction, almost against their will, a desperate giving in. Louie volunteered it, looked for it, delighted in it. Kissing her was a celebration, not a capitulation.

But tonight there was a tension. Louie put on some music and Willa watched her fiddle with the stereo and play a sixties revival group called The Burglars. She pulled the curtains across her ranchslider doors, then opened them again on the peaked ears and yellow eyes of Judas against the night. She was nervous, her hands moving jerkily, not with her usual ease. *The bed thing.*

Willa sat down on the floor beside the stereo. "They're good," she said. "Where'd you discover them?"

"Mo," Louie answered, joining her on the carpet. "She's always first to discover new bands."

They listened to the whole CD, and didn't talk much. Louie came over eventually and leaned against Willa's shoulder. Soon Willa noticed her breathing had taken on the regular rhythm of sleep. She shifted and Louie sat up.

"Louie, you're tired."

"No, no I'm not," and Willa saw her eyes flick across the room towards the beds. "Let's listen to something else. I'm not ready to go to bed yet."

Willa sighed. "I know."

Louie looked up at her tone.

"Relax, huh? I'm not expecting to sleep with you."

Louie dipped her head and fingered the carpet. "It's not that," she mumbled. "It's   it's the opposite. I don't want you to get into the other bed."

Neither of them went to bed. Louie found some matches and they lit candles. All night they lay on the floor, listening to music, talking quietly, touching each other. Louie was shy, Willa scared they would get caught, and both hesitant at first. The moon snailed across the window and shone on their bodies as they wrapped around each other, discarded clothes, fingered, kissed and discovered the other and themselves. Willa pulled the duvets and pillows from the beds and for a while they slept in each other's arms.

As the room grew light, Willa woke and looked at Louie asleep beside her. Her tousled hair lay still for once, black half-circles strewn across the pillow. The light sculpted her face so that her cheekbones and nose, the moulding of her lips and her jaw stood out, and Willa wished she had some poetry, some of Louie's own words to describe her loveliness. She'd thrown her leg out from under the cover and it lay next to Willa's, olive against her own pale calf. She thought of Cathy and their fearful touching, the denial afterwards and she shook her head in wonder. Willa smiled gratefully at Louie's sleeping face. This then, was what it was like to be in love, and to have it returned.

Louie stirred and woke slowly, then suddenly she jumped up and grabbed her watch.

"Take it easy, it's only seven," said Willa.

Louie sighed and flopped back down.

"Come with me," said Willa, helping her back up.

When Susi came in at eight o'clock, ostensibly to offer tea or coffee, she found both girls sound asleep in their own beds. Something similar to but not quite the same as disappointment passed across her face.

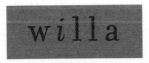

# willa

It was Saturday night and all hands on deck at the bar. Two of their staff were away including Midge who did meals. So Willa was doing a turn behind the Golden Grill with Jolene who dashed back and forth to help Sid when the bar traffic was heavy. Usually Willa avoided the pub—years of drunks and fights, vomiting and bad singing had put her off for life, but there were occasional times, and this was one of them, when the crowd were good-spirited, and the atmosphere full of *bonhomie,* when Willa laughed with them and liked them all.

"That should give you some legs, Bruce," she commented to a student as she handed him a T-bone steak and chips.

"What's wrong with m'legs?" he said, acting offended, and another guy gave him a playful shove.

"Too much sitting on your butt in that rust-bucket of yours rooting the clutch." It was Darryl, the mechanic from across the road.

"Don't you call my car a rust-bucket or I'll take my money elsewhere."

"Money? No money in clutch repairs, mate, they're fiddly as buggery."

"Oh, pull the other one," laughed Willa, "you garage people have got more money than you know what to do with. Our best customers, mechanics." Willa left them to the ensuing debate and threw more chips in the deep fryer.

"You're in fine form tonight," commented Jolene. "Had a good day?"

"Yeah, not bad at all."

"You're happy at the new school, love?" Jolene put her arm around her daughter's waist.

Willa smiled back. "Yeah, Mum, I like it." They went back to their work for a bit, then Willa said, "I'm going to be in the school production—Shakespeare."

"You're joking." Jolene put down her knife and looked delighted.

"Well, not acting. I'm doing the lights. Thought it might be a laugh."

"It's a start. We'll get you on the boards yet." Willa knew it was a disappointment to Jolene that neither of her daughters showed any inclination to sing or perform like their parents.

Later, she said, out of the blue, "Your friend Louie, is she in the production too?"

Willa stiffened. "Yeah, she is. She's one of the leads." *Is it that obvious?*

Jolene nodded. "She's a nice kid, Louie."

"Yeah, she is." *Nice*, she thought. *Yeah, like the Sahara's cosy at this time of year. She's nice to the power of a hundred! She's nice with turbo-charge and electric fuel injection! Nice, hell.*

Willa smiled as she thought about Louie today, rushing into Willa's home room at lunchtime and pulling her aside.

"Look, look," she'd said, shoving a book under Willa's nose. "Read this."

"What?" Willa had frowned at the tiny print. It was a very old, musty-smelling book.

"Here!" Louie pointed at the print and read out loud. *"It loved to happen."* She turned over the book, to show Willa the spine. "Marcus Aurelius. He was a Roman Emperor and philosopher. *It loved to happen,*" she repeated. "Isn't that it? What you were saying to Mum the other night? You know," she insisted when Willa must have looked blank. Louie lowered her voice. "About love and everything. You said it just happens, it isn't something you plan for or know about. It comes from outside and changes everything. *It loved to happen.* Like you and me."

The warmth of the crowd at the Duke increased as the temperature dropped outside. Not long after the Golden Grill closed for the night, someone came in and announced it was snowing. People milled out into the road and played in the white flurries, then hopped back inside for a drink. Sid was worried they'd run out of whisky.

Willa was as excited as anyone. She rushed through the last of the dishes in the kitchen, then headed out of the bar. "I'm going for a walk," she said to her mother.

"Hang on Willa, love," Jolene stopped her. "Where are you going? It's late to be out walking alone."

"Just a little way, to enjoy the snow—come on Mum, everyone's outside."

"Put on some warm clothes—really warm, I mean, and I suppose you're going to Louie's, are you?"

Willa was surprised into telling the truth. "Yes."

"Okay," agreed Jolene, and Willa noticed a little concerned frown around her eyes even though she was smiling. "I just like to know you're safe, you know?"

Willa was so excited and thankful she hugged her mother. Jolene's arms tightened about her, strong and wiry. "Be careful," she whispered, without explanation. When she pulled away Willa saw her mother blink rather hard, and she was sorry she hadn't been able to hug her since the Cathy mess.

"Off you go then," croaked Jolene, "boots, hat, scarf and gloves, all right?"

"Got it." She rushed up the stairs, chose a concoction of woollen garments, bundled most of her hair under a knitted hat and threw a heavy black coat over the rest. On her duchess sat an unopened blue envelope. It had arrived that afternoon. Willa looked at it for a minute, then poked out her tongue and threw it in the bin. She galloped down the stairs and Judas barked in excitement as they took off down the street. He zig-zagged about, sniffing and tossing the snow with his nose, his back legs skidding as he bounded back and forth.

"Wow! Big spin out, Judas," Willa laughed as the dog slid across the road until he was facing back the way he had come. There were no cars about and the snow lay several centimetres thick already. It was still and the streets had that magical hushed quality of snow at night. The bush beyond the road hung silent and hunched, gleaming under its cover of white.

She met Louie coming down the hill, a dark rustling lump in the mauve light, something waving like antlers on her head. "Hail, who goes there?" cried Louie. "On guard!" She came at Willa with a long karaka spear which Judas barked and jumped up at. The antlers, Willa realised, bending over with laughter, were actually the peaks of a large felt jester's hat.

"You look ridiculous," snorted Willa.

"Thank you. It's what I do best. Come Judas, let us ignoreth the slings and arrows of outrageous bores and cavorteth together in the snow."

Willa ran after her and tripped Louie up, then they bumped off each other in their swad of clothes, threw snowballs and pushed each other over. Louie tried capers and somersaults but Judas leapt on top of her and trampled her with his wet paws. Soon they were joined by some more people, including Mo and her brother Jay. Mo had brought some huge plastic bags and they made a scraping sound careering down the hill on them while Judas chased and cut them off, causing a pile-up at the bottom.

One by one the others went home, and when Mo and Jay disappeared, Louie, Willa and Judas went up to Louie's house. They'd taken to coming and going through the sliding doors into Louie's bedroom, so the Angelos didn't always know. They crept in quietly and tried to get warm in front of Louie's heater, but Judas always managed to get in front of them.

"What we need is a spa," said Louie after a while, looking at her snow-encrusted mittens.

"Mmm." Willa's black coat was dripping on the carpet. Warm water sounded wonderful. "Push *off*, Judas."

Louie jumped up. "Well, why not? A spa! A spa! My bedroom for a spa! I'm going to turn it on."

"But it's outside—well, mostly." In fact it had three walls and a roof, only the fourth wall being open to trees and the bush. "And your parents . . ."

"So what? We're just having a spa. If they ask, we tell the truth—we met down the street in the snow." Louie shrugged, her palms spread heavenwards like her father.

That's exactly what happened. Just as they were really enjoying the hot frothing water, and watching Judas's puzzlement at the snowflakes drifting down right beside them, in walked Susi in her dressing gown. Louie was in the process of fixing the clip that held Willa's hair up on the top of her head.

"What's going on? Oh—Willa," she feigned surprise. Judas woofed, once. "I didn't know you were here." She pulled her hands above the range of Judas's inquisitive nose and looked at her daughter. "Do you know what the time is, Louie?"

Louie's dark eyes sent a private message to Willa as she let go her hair. "Yes Mum, we asked Mr. Wolf and he said it was late. But look, it's snowing outside! Everyone's playing on the street.

I met Willa and we came back here for a spa. Isn't it amazing out there?"

Susi looked at both of them rather hard. Willa was pleased the bubbles hid her naked body. All the same, she was beginning to feel flushed. She drew up her legs and hugged her knees. Judas lay down with a small whine.

"Won't your mother be wondering where you are, Willa?" Susi enquired.

"No, I told her."

"I thought you said you only met on the street?"

"We did," said Willa. "But I thought—we might come back here."

"I see." Susi lifted an eyebrow and looked down at them grimly. "Well, I think it's time you went home."

"Mum!" objected Louie.

"It's late," Susi said.

"It's Saturday night."

"It's Sunday morning actually, and we've got church in seven hours."

"I'm not going," said Louie.

"Well the rest of this family is. And your father and I can't sleep with the noise of the spa motor."

"But—"

"Lou," Willa shook her head slightly.

Louie sighed in exasperation. "All right, you win. Do you think we could at least have some privacy to get dressed?"

Susi twisted her mouth. "Yes." As she went back through the door she turned to them a final time. "You're more than welcome to visit during the day, Willa, even with your dog," she said with the now familiar Antarctic smile, "but we all need our sleep, including Louie."

Willa smiled wanly in reply and the door closed. Louie exploded out of the pool.

74

"How dare she! What a bitch! You'd think I was twelve years old. God, Willa, I can't stand it when she's like that to you."

Willa stayed in the pool and closed her eyes.

"I don't know why. She's never been like this before. She just—"

"She knows, Lou."

Louie looked at Willa, her mouth still open. "What?"

"She knows. Something, anyway. She's suspicious of me."

"Do you think so?"

"Uhuh."

Louie was quiet for a moment, patting Judas's head and looking out at the falling snow. "She asked the other morning too, after you'd been here. She thought she heard voices in the middle of the night..."

"What did you say?"

"The truth, that you'd called in after the late shift at Burger Giant."

Willa thought again how different Louie was from Cathy, who had panicked and lied to her parents about everything, until she was so consumed with the deceit that it took over. She looked up. Louie had turned to face Willa, her dark curls shimmying against the backdrop of feathery snow. She absently noted that Louie's hair was almost blue-black, metallic like starlings' wings.

"What should we do?" she asked.

Willa grinned. "Put some clothes on. I can't think straight."

Louie tossed her a towel. "That's because you're not."

# louie

Both Louie and Willa had to fit the rehearsals for *Twelfth Night* around their jobs at Burger Giant. For Willa, it wasn't hard— she was only needed for a couple of early rehearsals, then took Louie and some others for fencing sessions at lunchtime. But Louie had to be at most practices, and they took up her after-school hours, weekends, and, as the deadline approached, evenings as well. Then Willa got involved again, setting up and operating the lighting. They'd both had to ask Kevin to give them a couple of weeks' leave.

That left some time at least for Louie to learn her lines. Willa knew them already—sitting up in the lighting box she'd learnt virtually the entire play by heart, and Louie teased her that she was hoping Mo would fall sick on opening night and Willa could play Orsino.

Willa denied it, but Louie knew she was a little jealous of Mo. Not only was she Louie's closest "ordinary" friend, but she was playing the Duke Orsino who falls in love with Viola in the play, and that led to some extraordinary moments in rehearsal.

A week or so from opening night, Mrs. Ashton was having terrible trouble showing Mo how to fake a stage kiss by sweeping Viola in her arms away from the audience, bending her backwards and leaning over her face. Mo kept getting her footwork all muddled and in exasperation Mrs. Ashton, who was halfway up a ladder fixing a curtain motioned to Willa, who was often standing around ready to fill in for absent actors.

"For goodness' sake, Willa, show her what I mean. Just take her weight with your right arm and swing her round."

Louie paused to take a sip of her Coke as Willa leapt lightly onto the stage and walked over. She deftly slipped an arm around Louie and leaned her backwards dramatically. Centimetres from her face she murmured, "Kiss Mo and I'll black the lights."

Mrs. Ashton crowed from above, "See? It's easy. Don't even think about your feet!"

What Willa didn't know was that Mo was a bit jealous of Willa, too. Most days Willa and Louie had taken to walking home together, and although Louie tried to encourage Mo to join them, she usually made an excuse. More than any of her friends it was Mo who had noticed the difference in Louie. She made little comments about not wanting to get in the way, or to bother her. She'd taken to ringing before visiting, just to check that it was all right. Louie knew she was mostly checking to see if Willa was there. In her own quiet, noncomplaining way, Louie thought, Mo was backing off. Now they were in the play together it was different though. Mo and Louie had been friends since the third form, and had acted together in plays for nearly five years, including pieces they wrote for fun and performed at school, like the Comedy Club. There was always a special closeness when they worked together. The day of the stage kiss, Willa stayed behind to rig up a couple of extra spotlights so Louie made a point of walking home only with Mo. She knew Mo was hurt and she wanted to explain what was happening, but she wasn't sure if she could.

"Willa's good at the lighting, eh?" said Mo, as they cut through the park. It was five o'clock and the birds were chirping and bustling about the trees all around them.

"Yep," answered Louie, thinking, *It's not fair. I have to tell her.*

"You like her a lot, don't you?"

"Mo . . . I—" Louie went blank.

"I'm sorry, Louie, dumb question. I don't mind, really. I don't have to be your best friend. Just—a good friend, okay?"

Louie stopped and stared straight up at an enormous kowhai tree. It was just in blossom and tuis had been feeding on it as she and Willa walked past this morning. Now it was empty, the late sun firing its flowers like a chandelier of golden droplets. *Help me say this right,* she asked the tree silently.

"You're still my best friend, Mo," Louie said carefully. "Willa's not a friend." She stared at Mo for a long time and waited. Mo's eyes narrowed, puzzled.

"What d'you mean?"

"She's—more than a friend." *There, it's said. Think what you like.*

Mo was still frowning at Louie. She tilted her head to one side, and gradually a small stunned smile appeared. She opened her mouth slowly. "You mean . . ." She stopped and let her mouth drop completely open in amazement. Louie began to smile back, a little at a time, terrified, hopeful. It was almost as hard as it had been facing up to Willa in the first place.

Mo was shaking her head and staring wordlessly at Louie. "I had no idea!" she finally said. "I mean, you and Willa. *You* and *Willa!* Louie—" She took a step forward, then stopped and put both hands on top of her head, comically. "I just never knew. How could I have never known?"

Louie shrugged back at her. "*I* never knew. Well, not properly. It just—happened. Mo, what do you think? Really?"

Mo still looked stunned. "Hell, Louie, don't ask me. I mean, I think it's . . . fine—I think." She frowned and snorted and frowned again, then grinned at Louie and shrugged. "Didn't you fancy me?"

Louie rolled her eyes. "No, I didn't." She noticed Mo had gone

78

quite pink after that question, so walked over and linked arms with her. "In fact, the only other person I fancied was—don't tell a soul—Mrs. Ashton."

Mo laughed out loud and they began walking again. "Oh, Louie, everyone's got a crush on Mrs. Ashton, that's nothing special."

A little bit further on she stopped suddenly. "No wonder she was able to do that stage kiss so well. I thought she was a bit pleased with herself!"

"Exactly."

"Lou," Mo smiled curiously, "what's it like? No!" she quickly held up a hand, "don't tell me. I don't want to know."

Louie walked on a bit without speaking, trying not to smile to herself so obviously. Eventually she looked up and Mo was staring at her intently.

"Well?"

"It's dynamite, Mo. It's dynamite."

# louie

The thing about acting, for Louie, was that she wasn't. She wasn't conscious, that is, that she was acting. When everything came together, and she finally knew her lines and moves, she became the character, and it was as if she was saying those lines as she thought them, making those moves because she had to, feeling what she did in response to other characters as if she'd never heard their lines before. The distant murmur as the audience gathered on the night, the old-fashioned putty smell of greasepaint combined with sweat, deodorant and musty costumes in the dressingrooms, the oily thick feel of the make-up on her face, the nervous reciting of lines, the occasional explosion of panic as a hat or stage letter couldn't be found . . . the edginess of those final minutes excited Louie tremendously, but it was what happened on stage that mattered most. When she walked out onto the now brilliant set and felt the hot lights and the dark quivering presence of the audience, Louie's blood rose until she pulsed with power and brightness and held the eyes of the audience like a magnet. Other actors' nervousness was there in their eyes, flicking desperately as they tried to remember each line and move ahead of time, but for Louie her heartbeat slowed, her breathing calmed and the performance flowed out of her better than ever it did in rehearsal.

Mrs. Ashton had told her once she was a real actor—"you're more yourself on stage than off."

In that first night performance Louie felt that power and played up to it, tossing the odd line or expression to the audience for an extra laugh, heightening the comedy where she could, the passion when she talked of love to Orsino, the sadness when she spoke of the brother she thought was dead. At the end the audience clapped and whistled their approval as she stood forward, hands linked with Mo, and bowed.

"You were terrific, you were wonderful!" cried Willa, a rush of red hair flying backstage as she joined Mrs. Ashton in hugging everyone. Louie waited for her turn. "You especially," Willa said to her quietly. "Unbelievable."

None of them wanted to go home, so they took their time getting changed and setting their costumes and props for the next night, talking all the time about the performance. "Did you see Dena's face when I mucked up that line?" "What about Rosa— 'Unwretched grace'!" "What?" "She said 'Unwretched grace' instead of 'ungracious wretch'!" "And Mo's shoe! Remember when her shoe came off?" "Oh, god yes," said Louie, "Talk about ticklish. It was like putting it back on a jack hammer!"

It was hard to sleep that night. Louie was so hyped she ran through all her lines as she lay in bed. When she found she was starting over again, she got up and dressed.

She didn't often go to Willa's place at night because it was harder to get in, but she enjoyed the walk anyway. It was still and cool and all Louie could hear was her own breath and the scrape of her shoes on the pavement.

The Duke was in darkness, and Louie stood for a while gazing up, thinking about Willa, about this thing she'd got into. It made her feel special, set apart in some way to have this secret. Partly it was thrilling because it was secretive, full of meaningful glances and midnight assignations. Sometimes that made her frightened, like when she saw her mother's hostility to Willa, but mostly she felt excited and happy and lucky all at once. She wanted to share everything with Willa, every moment, every thought. When Willa wouldn't tell her something, like what the blue letters were that she kept getting, it drove Louie crazy.

Louie scrabbled around and found some small stones at the base of the fence. She threw three or four before one contacted with Willa's bedroom window and then the clatter was so loud she shrank behind the fence. A minute or so later, just when she was thinking about throwing another, the window squeaked open and Willa leaned out, Judas's nose beside her.

Louie waved and Willa made a sort of snorting noise, then disappeared. A few moments later the back door opened and Judas came nosing over to Louie who followed him inside.

Thursday night's performance wasn't quite as good—a couple of people lost their lines and the atmosphere was flatter. Mrs. Ashton cheered them though, saying they were the only ones who noticed and that the principal, Mrs. Eagles, had said she thought it was the best production yet. Jolene had gone that night too and afterwards, to Louie's delight, gave her a big hug.

"You keep acting, Beatnik," she said privately. "There's a big difference between music and theatre, I know. But if I was looking for a music star, I'd be looking for that quality you've got on stage. You were a delight to watch."

Most of them packed up quickly that night, and pleased though she was by Jolene's comment, Louie felt wiped out. All the rehearsals and tension, the nights Willa had stayed late pretending they were learning lines, not to mention last night at the Duke, had caught up on her. Susi didn't wake her to go to school the next morning and Louie slept solidly for twelve hours.

So when she and Willa arrived at the auditorium for the last of the three-night season, Louie was in good form. "My parents are coming tonight," she reminded Willa, and hoped silently that they would be as nice to Willa about her lighting as Jolene had been about her acting. She doubted it.

The final night was always the most popular. Most of the staff came, many of the parents and lots of their friends. Dena Mason was beside herself with horror when she spotted her boyfriend Greg in the audience. Willa seemed a bit unnerved too, and mentioned there were some oddbods in the crowd tonight, but Louie was too busy trying to sponge the brown greasepaint marks off her ruff to notice.

In fact the auditorium was full, and the buzz Louie noticed in the audience from the beginning was palpable. Within moments she knew that tonight she mustn't play to them—they were already overexcited—but pull in and keep control of the atmosphere.

And that was what it must be like for Viola all the time, she thought suddenly. Keeping control of herself and the situation was vital. Always lying, pretending to be a boy servant to Orsino when in fact she had fallen in love with him. The fabric of her existence threatened to fall apart should she let her true feelings show—she could be out of a job, a home, and have lost all chance of being with the one she loved. And it was also like her and Willa—hiding that secret that nevertheless bubbled and fizzed inside you, knowing that you loved where it was forbidden to love.

Louie's lines were just as perfect as the previous nights; her moves too were impeccable. But there was something extra tonight that she was only semi-conscious of—something in her expression and delivery, that made tears spring unexpectedly to eyes when she said:

*My father had a daughter loved a man...*
*...She never told her love,*
*But let concealment, like a worm i' the bud,*
*Feed on her damask cheek: she pined in thought,*

*And with a green and yellow melancholy*
*She sat like patience on a monument,*
*Smiling at grief. Was this not love indeed?*

The tenderness on Mo's face was genuine as she struggled to find Orsino's words to answer. Louie saw it, and captured it and Mo, keeping that feeling between them for the whole performance. At the end, as Dena sang the final notes of the Clown's song, there was a long breathless silence, then, like a string that the cast had been holding taut finally snapping, the audience exploded into rapturous applause. Mo's hand squeezed Louie's and they both stood forward and bowed. Louie knew without a doubt that it was her best performance ever.

It was after the flowers for Mrs. Ashton and several curtain calls that went on too long because of the stage manager's enthusiasm that Louie finally saw Willa. She rushed up to Louie first this time, forgetting the others, and threw her arms around her.

"I love you, Louie," she whispered.

As Louie opened her mouth to reply she caught sight of her parents and Marietta waiting at the door.

"Hi!" she said, knowing she was going bright red, but hoping the greasepaint would hide it. Willa let go and turned round.

"Hi," she said, and Louie lost all hope as she saw the colour Willa turned.

Susi spread her mouth in something that looked like but wasn't a smile and gave Louie a quick kiss. "Well done, Louie. You were very good, everyone said so."

Tony enveloped her in a hug and tried to make up for Susi. "You were fabulous. Nobody noticed anyone else on stage. They needn't have bothered. You were the star."

"Dad," Louie frowned as some other actors were coming in the dressing room.

"Well that's what I thought. I'm allowed to, I'm your father."

"Wasn't she wonderful?" asked a bouquet of flowers that squeezed in the door in front of Mrs. Ashton.

"She was brilliant," agreed Tony.

"And Willa's lighting? Wasn't that lovely? You did a super job, Willa. I don't know what we would have done without you. It's the work behind the scenes that people often forget about," she told Susi.

Susi smiled tightly. "I'm sure."

"Hello," said Mrs. Ashton. "Who's this? Are you Louie's sister?"

"I'm Ettie," answered Marietta. "I'm coming to Woodhaugh High next year."

"Really? Am I going to get to teach you drama too?"

"No," Marietta replied. "I'm into computers and cross country. I don't like plays."

Mrs. Ashton grinned. "We'll fix that."

Eventually Louie cleared her dressing room, but only after Susi said to her, "I'm afraid we don't have room for Willa if you're thinking of our giving her a lift."

"Mum!"

"Sorry, Louie, but there must be dozens of cars going her way. I'm sure she'll be able to get a lift with someone."

Louie stewed as she got changed and noticed the beginning of play crash coming on. It was over so quickly—three performances and you're done—and all that work and effort, the thrill and nerves, were over. The best performance she'd ever managed was already a memory. And all her mother could say was, you were very good and we can't take Willa home. Mo never got on as much of a high as Louie; neither did she fall prey to depressions afterwards. She packed up quickly and was already talking about her big hockey match tomorrow as she left. Louie took her time spreading cold cream over her face and wiping off the make-up. She exchanged a few jokes with the others, but her heart wasn't in it. All she could think of was that this was her last performance at this school, her last time working with Mrs. Ashton. She put everything away carefully in its place, taking home her costume to wash. She put her tatty script in her bag along with the programme as a memento and breathed in the smell of the dressing room for a last time.

Nearly everyone was gone. Louie walked across the stage once more. Tomorrow they would begin striking the set. She stood stage centre, feeling that familiar tiny but huge sensation as the air seemed to shimmer about her and echo with all the sound that wasn't there. It was just a stupid school hall, she knew that. But it was where she had felt the only thing as strong and as right as Willa. Louie looked up at the empty auditorium and gave it a silent thank you.

On the way home Susi seemed determined to talk about anything but the play. She asked Marietta what she thought about Woodhaugh High and mentioned that they might be taking her with them to Bali in the school holidays if she was lucky. Then she asked Tony what other package trips they could get and suggested they might all go, Louie and Nic included. Louie couldn't have cared less about going to Bali right then. It was only time away from Willa.

"Hey Mum, you know that thing you went to see tonight, at the school, in the hall, you know, what was it again?" she asked, exasperated.

"What do you mean, the play?"

"That's it," she clicked her fingers. "I thought you'd forgotten."

"No, Louie, we told you how good you were. You know we did."

"What about Mo?"

"She was good too."

Louie nodded slowly. "Okay. . . what about Dena?"

"Very good."

"Vika? Rosa? The scenery?"

"What is the matter with you? They were all good."

"Especially the scenery," chipped Tony.

"So haven't you anything to say about the play itself, or what you really thought?"

"Well," Susi shrugged a little in the front seat. Louie wished she could see her face. "It was a funny sort of a play to do, really. For a girls' school, I mean."

"What do you mean?"

"Well, all that, what do you call it—cross-dressing? Girls being boys falling in love with girls. It's a bit hard to believe."

Louie felt enormously irritated. This wasn't about the play.

"It's *Shakespeare*."

"I know that. But it is a bit out of date, isn't it? And Mrs. Ashton always seems to make you the boy. It's probably just as well you'll be at university next year. You'll get more scope."

"Girls' parts you mean."

"Well, yes." Susi turned and smiled at her. "You are a girl, after all!"

"In Shakespeare's time all the female parts were played by boys, you know," Louie said, focusing hard on the back of her mother's headrest. "And I *was* playing a female part, actually, in case you hadn't noticed. Viola is a woman."

"You know what I mean, Louie. She was pretending to be a boy for most of the play."

"I couldn't understand what they were saying," offered Marietta. "I mean, you were good, Louie, but the rest of it was boring."

"I didn't ask you," Louie said grumpily.

"Well I had to go, didn't I? I'm allowed an opinion. I thought it was dumb."

"That's because you're dumb."

"Now, now," Tony interrupted from the driving seat. "That's enough. Marietta, I saw you laughing lots of times."

"Yeah, I was laughing at Louie in those dorky tights."

"Just shut up, will you. You're pathetic." Louie kicked her sister's leg. She wanted to hit her harder, or punch a hole in the car window or something.

"This is why we couldn't take anyone else home. You're both tired and I knew there'd be a fight," said Susi.

"What do you mean, 'anyone?' It was Willa."

"It doesn't matter who it was," replied Susi, in her reasonable voice.

"Like hell," muttered Louie.

"Pardon?" Susi had turned around and looked directly at Louie.

Louie stared back at her angrily. Why did Susi keep pretending? Why did she keep confronting Louie about Willa in snide, sly ways to try and bait her into saying the one thing she didn't want to hear? She was on the verge of saying *You hate Willa because I love her,* but at the last minute she drew her legs up onto the seat and sank back into the leather. "Nothing," she answered, looking pointedly out the window.

"Get your feet off the seat," ordered Susi, and turned back to the front.

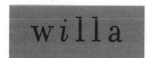
# willa

It was almost enough to throw her completely. Keith. Sitting nonchalantly in the bright blue seats, and with him, Kevin from Burger Giant. Kevin was wearing his usual work pants and leather jacket, Keith was in a dark suit and tie. What on earth were they doing there?

She knew they'd seen her before the play started, scuttling backstage and then up to the lighting box twice. She'd only met Keith's eyes the once, but his look was so direct, so full, that it was as if all the auditorium noise had died away and he'd stood and said, "Didn't expect me, did you?" During the interval he held himself self-consciously, aware of her eyes, turning his head slowly round the auditorium with a slight smile on his lips. He didn't resemble her of course, but his very presence was a reminder of Cathy, an old, painful feeling.

It worried Willa. She tried to put it out of her mind but it was strange. Back at work, Kevin teased Louie about the play for days, but he never mentioned Keith, and for some reason neither did Willa. Then, one night the following week, Keith turned up at Burger Giant.

It was late, almost midnight, and he walked straight up to her with the same small smile.

"Hello."

Willa found she couldn't look back at him straight. She didn't say anything.

"Bit of a change from a pub, isn't it?" He smiled fully at her now, and Willa frowned. He was wearing a suit again, and bright tie.

"Can I help you?"

"Cathy's brother."

"I know who you are." *Stepbrother, actually.*

"Still remember, then, do you?" he asked coolly. "So do I."

Willa's shoulders tightened. "What do you want, Keith?"

He raised his eyebrows and looked at the board above. "A Coke, and regular french fries."

As she filled his order, Kevin appeared. He greeted Keith with a clap on the shoulder and they started talking cars and stereos. Willa followed their conversation, noting that Keith, unlike Kevin, actually knew what he was talking about. She handed his order over the counter.

"Hey, it's on the house," insisted Kevin, putting his hand over the register to stop Willa charging him. "Just tell me about that natty little four wheel drive out there, what type's that?"

"Rav 4," said Willa, when Keith hesitated.

Kevin turned to her, surprised. "Since when did you know about cars?"

She shrugged, wishing she hadn't said anything.

"Keith's in car sales you know," Kevin told Willa. "He's going to get me a good deal. What's the name of your rip-off place?"

"Mannix Motors, on the main drag."

Willa went cold. That was the car sales across the road from the Duke. "I didn't know that," she said.

Keith just lifted his eyebrows.

"You wouldn't warrant it, you were such a dunce at school, mate," offered Kevin cheerfully. He took Keith off to a table out

90

of hearing, where they sat and laughed, glancing occasionally at Willa.

"What's with Mr. Up-Himself?" asked Joan, making a face. "Found himself a friend?"

"Looks like it," replied Willa. She emptied the last of the chips from the warmer.

"Must be desperate." Joan stared at Keith. "Mmm, nice tie," she said, and giggled. "Bet his mum chose it for him!"

Willa tried not to think about Keith's mum, but a flash of trap-door mouth and accusing eyes shot through her. She slopped water in the warmer and began scrubbing. Kevin and Keith were watching and she was aware of her face going red in the steam, her hair straggling out from the clips and paper hat, and of her breasts moving in time with the scrubbing.

Joan stacked the plates and lowered her voice. "Hey, Deirdre reckons there's something wrong with Kevin, the way he goes on. She said those that talk about it, don't do it. She thinks Kevin's in denial."

"What?"

"Kevin," she said, nodding towards their table. "She reckons he's a poof, just doesn't know it. Eh," she came over, snorting with suppressed laughter, "maybe that's his boyfriend. Old mummy's boy in his flash suit. Certainly looks the type."

Willa had breathed in too much steam from inside the cabinet and everything went white. She tried to pull out quickly and banged her head on the door. The water splashed somewhere, her feet slipped, then there was a crash and she was on the floor.

"Willa! Ooh, shit, are you all right?"

Joan was trying to pull her up, but her elbow hurt where she'd landed. Willa sat for a moment on the ground, then slowly picked herself up as Kevin and Keith appeared. Kevin cracked a joke but then he saw her face and looked worried. He took her arm gently and examined it. Over his shoulder Willa caught Keith's eye and he gave her a sheepish grin.

"Should I take her in to Accident and Emergency?" asked Joan, who had got some ice and handed it to her.

Willa pulled her arm from Kevin's grasp and wrapped the ice bag round her elbow. "It's okay, really. Just a thump."

"You sure?" Kevin asked. "You went down like a sack of spuds."

"I could take you in," offered Keith, concerned.

*Stop being nice to me,* thought Willa. "No, please. It's feeling better already. Just the funny bone, you know?" She grinned painfully at Joan. "Must've been your jokes."

It was knocking-off time anyway. Willa sat down with a drink and ignored Keith while Kevin finished the cabinet and Joan washed the floor. They all wanted to drive her home but she insisted she needed the fresh air and Judas needed the walk. All the way home in the dark streets she saw Keith's face, and then Cathy's, their mother's, their father's. And she saw Mrs. Angelo's face, with that wary, closed expression. Dare she go through it all again? The lights were off at the pub, everything closed up. Willa gave Judas a bowl of water and to the sound of his glock glock glock she went straight to bed and cried.

The next day she told Louie.

"It's just—like I can't escape the past, eh. Keith's not even horrible, he's just—there. How long before he tells Kevin about me and Cathy?"

"Hey, who cares what Kevin thinks. He's a dropkick, anyway." Louie stretched out on the sofa with a sandwich.

"You wouldn't care?"

Louie looked at her in surprise. "No." But her eyes slid away.

Willa got up and walked around the room fiddling with things. There was a display case of blue Venetian glass that was placed to catch the light. Willa watched the white light settle like water on the round edges.

"Has your mum mentioned Bali again?" she asked lightly.

Louie shifted on the couch. "Yep. We had argument number two last night. Final points, me twenty, her none, but she still wins. This house is a logic-free zone, honestly." She took a bite of her sandwich and talked with her mouth full. "Apparently I'm not old enough to stay here on my own. Even though Nic did," she added. "She complains one minute that I'm not working hard enough on schoolwork, that I'm not spending much time on netball or debating and the next minute she wants to whisk me away overseas for three weeks."

Willa stared through a bowl into the view outside, making the bush dark blue like thunder clouds. "She doesn't trust you, eh. With me."

"Tell me about it," said Louie. "It's a mission. Destroy Willa, the Alien from Planet Duke. She's always poking around, asking questions, trying to catch me out. There are these little suspicious sparks that bounce off her every time she walks into my room."

"Well, she's right, isn't she. You are hiding something from her."

Louie had been about to say something else, but she stopped and went silent. Willa moved her eye down a glass to its narrow base and watched the blue world outside go from very big to very small. "Maybe you'd be better just to go to Bali."

"I don't want to go!" Louie sounded petulant, like a child. "Why should I go on an expensive holiday when I just want to stay here?" Her voice softened. "With you."

Willa smiled at the blue world and turned to Louie. "I don't want you to go, either. I just thought it might help get your mother off your case."

That night Willa left Judas at the pub and crept round the back of the Metal Petal to where Louie had left her sliding doors open.

She took off her clothes and slipped into bed beside Louie and held her tight. She knew Louie wasn't going to win the argument with Susi. In less than a fortnight it would be the holidays and Louie would be gone for three whole weeks. Willa was shocked at how much the thought upset her. She stroked Louie's arm, her back, her long thigh, she kissed her passionately. Louie threw off her tee shirt and wound herself around Willa. Her skin was smooth and warm, there seemed to be a layer of electricity between them. Louie held Willa's long hair off her face and kissed her eyes, her cheeks, her lips. A tide rose within them and in the darkness Willa saw shadowy angles of arm, shoulder, hip, knee. Their love-making was wild and silent, heightened by the edge of grief.

They slept for a while afterwards, before Willa awoke, cold. She pulled the cover over Louie and began to get dressed. The bedside clock read 1:34.

"Don't go," murmured Louie.

"Have to."

She sat up in bed. "It's raining."

Willa tied her boots, and glanced at the window.

"Have you got an umbrella?" asked Louie.

"I don't mind getting wet."

"Take an umbrella. Please?" Louie leaned over and kissed her. Willa's brain began to fizz.

"Okay."

"There's about twenty in the stand by the back door. Never know when a busload of needy wet people might turn up. Just take any, no one'll miss it."

Willa hated moving around the house at night—usually she wouldn't even go to the toilet, which Louie found hilarious. "Do you think they can tell it's your pee?" she laughed. Tony and Susi slept upstairs so Willa would be safe going as far as the back door.

Or so she thought. As Willa slipped along the hall she suddenly heard a swish of material and saw a dense shape on the stairs. She side-stepped lightly into the living room. To her horror the shadow came through another door into the same room, and the light from the windows lit her up clearly. Mrs. Angelo. Willa fled behind a pillar, then ladybird-stepped carefully round it to keep out of vision as Susi walked across the room with a glass in her hand. Then Willa ducked down behind a large rolled armchair and prayed Susi couldn't hear her heart gunning like a Harley Davidson.

Susi turned on a table lamp and fossicked in the magazine stand. Eventually, just when Willa thought her strangulated breathing had to give her away, she heard a click and the lamp was out. The darkness was blinding for a few seconds, then she saw the door swing closed behind Susi Angelo.

Willa took two deep breaths then stood up. She felt so shaky she collapsed in the chair she'd hidden behind, her mouth still wide open in disbelief. It was just changing into a grin when the door opened a second time, and Mrs. Angelo reentered.

This time Willa was caught in full view. She froze, sitting like a corpse with its mouth open. Susi walked straight over to the table with the lamp and as Willa held her breath, Mrs. Angelo reached down and picked up her glass of water with a tut-tut sound. She turned and walked back out the door again without, unbelievably, seeing Willa right in front of her.

# louie

She'd never really lied to her family before. She liked her family, actually. They were kind to her, they were proud of her, they wanted to believe everything she told them. Now she was playing her father against her mother; he trusted her word, Susi didn't. Now she was saying Marietta had a nightmare—that's why Susi heard voices in the night. Now she blamed Nic for leaving doors unlocked at odd times. She used her other friends as covers for spending more and more time with Willa, and she let Marietta insinuate she was keen on Mo's brother Jay, to keep Susi off the track.

And slowly, Louie felt sick.

She tried to go to church, to regain something of a sense of family, of trust, of being the daughter they always thought she was. But she found herself staring at the limp, crucified Jesus and thinking of Willa squinting at the picture of Jesus at home and shaking her head. The laughter bubbled inside her and she saw the church through Willa's eyes—all the ornamentation, the priest in a frock, the standing, sitting, kneeling, reciting congregation like an obedient flock of sheep. Still, the feeling in the church, the feeling behind the words and the ritual and the people singing together meant something to Louie. It had always made her feel opened up inside, somehow, like the painting of Jesus, his heart exposed, pulsing on the outside of his body. Now it flooded her with feeling for Willa. She wanted to cry out how wonderful this thing was, how overwhelmingly happy it made her to be in love. But the guilt at having to hide it from her family was overwhelming too. She stared at the Christ in a huge confusion of feeling and could only say over and over again, "please, *please*." Then the priest, the nice young, new priest talked of family, of openness, of love. He asked them all to turn to each other and greet them in the name of God. Louie smiled weakly and shook hands with Nic, with Marietta, with Tony, with Susi, with Bernadette and Martin from down the road, with Shaun and Pam who'd been to dinner the other night, and they all said to each other, "Peace be with you, peace be with you." It sounded like the whole church was murmuring "baaa baaa baaa."

At the door they stopped to talk with the new young priest, Father Campion. He nodded and smiled and asked them politely about their forthcoming holiday to Bali. Louie looked at her feet while her father answered, and noticed something odd about Father Campion. He had on running shoes under his vestments, quite shabby old Reeboks. She looked up to see him following her gaze. He smiled at her, secretly, mischievously.

At home the Metal Petal was cold and unwelcoming. All the underfloor heating in the world couldn't make the large open spaces cosy on a wet day. Louie longed for a small room, with comfortable furniture and no flow. She fantasised about being with Willa in a cabin in the mountains, drinking soup and snuggling up in front of a log fire. Instead, the ceiling eye lights stared at her accusingly and Susi told her to get her feet off the couch.

"Why don't you start organising your clothes for Bali? There must be things that need a wash," her mother suggested.

"I'm not coming to Bali."

Susi snapped the kettle on to boil. "Don't be silly, Louie. It's all booked."

"So unbook it. You own the travel agency."

"It's too late. You know all this."

"I never agreed to come," Louie said angrily. "Why take me on a holiday I don't want to go on? What a waste of money."

"You'll enjoy it once you're there."

Louie was cold and hurt and fed up. "You just want to get me away from Willa."

The air went tight. Louie felt a rush of adrenalin. She'd said it.

"Don't you think that might be a good idea?" answered Susi in a careful tone. "You do spend an awful lot of time together."

"No!" yelled Louie. "No we don't! We don't spend nearly enough time together, and you've no right to try and separate us. It's pathetic!"

She was in tears, on her feet, shouting, hardly aware of the shock on her mother's face. Louie rushed from the room, down the hall, slammed the doors and plunged onto her bed sobbing. "It's too hard," she cried into the duvet, "it's too bloody hard."

Okay, it was an overreaction of the first degree, but Louie didn't recover from tantrums quickly. Even when the anger was gone and she just felt drained and numb, she couldn't face anyone. She played music in her room, and made forays for food when the others weren't around. Her father asked her if she wanted to go with him to a film festival movie, but she put him off. Marietta pestered her to time her run around the block and she grumped at her sister to go away. Louie badly wanted to talk to someone who understood, but Willa was working until 11 P.M. Mo? Louie still didn't feel easy discussing it with her. Mention of the "relationship" always made Mo go slightly pink. She decided to wait it out and hope Willa turned up after work.

She did. Louie was sitting up in bed pretending to work on an Art History essay when Willa appeared at the ranchslider. The sight of her was such a relief Louie started to cry almost immediately.

"What's up?"

"It's stupid. I had a huge row with Mum, about Bali, about you."

"Uh-oh."

"No, she doesn't know anything," Louie said. As she explained she looked at Willa's kind, safe face, and wondered how anyone could dislike her. It seemed so simple, so right when she was there.

Louie was so wound up she gabbled about everything for over an hour. Willa listened patiently. Finally Louie was silent.

"Dare truth or promise," said Willa.

"Truth."

"You always say truth. Okay, are you afraid that if you go away I'll change my mind about you?"

"No. Maybe. A little."

"I won't. You know I won't." Willa's opal eyes held hers, clear and light.

"Promise."

"Promise. If you promise to go and enjoy it and come back all brown and beautiful."

She was right, Louie thought, a trip to Bali was hardly a punishment. But it made her want to hold onto Willa now. She convinced Willa to slip off her bulky winter clothes and hop into bed. "I can't stay," Willa said again, as Louie fingered her camisole.

"Where do you get this sexy underwear? It's very unfair of you to tease me like this. It's wickedness. I'm sure the Bible says something about naughty underwear being the cloth of the Devil. He's always in that slinky red satin number..." Louie lay back on the pillow, still talking. Willa's beautiful face hung above her and her tiny cool hands began to stroke Louie's forehead. She knew what that meant. It meant she was raving, but if she kept talking maybe she could keep Willa there a little longer.

"You look tired," Willa said. "Close your eyes and I'll talk to you for a change." Louie did as she was told and had just felt Willa's lips touch her eyelids when the door burst open.

Susi.

louie

"Get out of there. *Get out.*"

Her mother's eyes were fixed on Willa and her voice was quiet and shaking.

"When I come back into this room, I want you gone, I want those doors *locked,*" her eyes flicked angrily to Louie for a second then back to Willa, "and I don't want to see you again. Do you understand?"

Louie looked at Willa, who had jumped out of bed and was holding her jacket around her middle. Her knuckles were white, like her cheekbones, and her red hair hung in ropes. "Yes," she whispered, and they watched as Susi closed the door and disappeared.

Louie sank under the covers, her hands over her face. Willa was frantically throwing on her jeans and jersey.

"Oh god, oh god, oh god," she was repeating in a sort of wail. Louie dragged her hands down her face until they splayed on either side of her open mouth. She caught sight of herself in the reflection of the ranchslider, looking like Munch's painting *The Scream.*

What could she say? Like the night on Signal Hill when Willa had first touched her, Louie was paralysed. She knew she should say something, something reassuring, but she just watched as Willa grabbed her boots, perched on the bed, changed her mind and sat on the floor to pull them on. She jumped up, snatched her jacket from the ground and threw it around her. Then she turned to Louie.

Suddenly she was there by her side, pulling Louie's scream off her face. "It'll be all right," she was saying. "It'll be all right." Louie still couldn't answer. She felt Willa's small hands cup her face, then they were gone. "I love you, Lou." Her voice cracked and she frowned, leapt up and strode outside, sliding the door behind her.

Louie drew up her legs, hugged her knees, and stared at the place where Willa had disappeared. In the dark glass doors she saw a girl in a white bed, sheets drawn around her. She was trapped in the cold, black glass, she was somewhere else, not on the other side, but inside the glass, in a thin layer of ice and you could only see her from one angle, otherwise she disappeared.

There was a soft knock at her bedroom door and Susi appeared. She sat on the side of the bed and gave her a hot drink. She murmured words of reassurance, she smiled like a mother, she patted her arm. She made noises for a long time; once she sounded stern and forced Louie to look at her, but it hurt Louie's eyes. They were hot and burning, so she looked back into the icy glass where it was cool and there was no reflection of a mother.

After a long time Susi tucked things around Louie, locked the ranchslider, pulled the curtains and turned out the light. As soon as she was gone Louie got out of bed and drew the curtains apart. The black ice sighed and invited her in properly. It was deeper now, it moved like water, like oily seaweed and its patterns mesmerised her.

willa

She hung around outside the house until she saw Louie's light go out, then trudged back to the Duke. It was freezing. She didn't cry, not this time. She worried.

All was quiet at the pub. At least that meant Mrs. Angelo hadn't rung Jolene. Willa hugged Judas on her bed, and lay awake worrying about Louie, wanting to phone, wanting Louie to phone her, knowing neither would happen.

Early in the morning Willa went back to Louie's street to meet her going to school. She hid behind some trees across the road, and watched Tony Angelo leave in the Mercedes, with Marietta. There was no sign of Louie, or of Mrs. Angelo. Eventually Willa went to school, where she fretted and panicked every time a message came to the class. Nothing happened.

Nothing happened that night either. Willa checked, but Louie's ranchslider was closed and there was no light. She didn't dare go any closer.

As the days passed Willa felt colder inside. This was the last thing she'd expected—no word. She went to work at Burger Giant and was asked to take over Louie's shift. It seemed someone had called Kevin. The official line both there and at school was that Louie was sick, and Willa had no idea if anyone knew otherwise.

102

When Mo asked her, Willa told the truth—she hadn't seen or heard from Louie for three days.

"She'll probably see the term out, I s'pose. Only two more days."

Willa nodded. "I guess."

Willa was prepared to do anything for Louie, but she had to know. Each day she arrived at school expectant, fearful, hoping and dreading to see Louie. When the last day of term passed with still no sign of her, Willa could take it no longer. She stood outside the Metal Petal that night, Judas by her side, clenching and unclenching her hands, only partly to keep them warm. The frost had already settled on the few cars on the street and Willa's careful steps seemed to echo in the stillness. It was 1 A.M. Finally Willa threw a small stone at Louie's ranchslider. It missed by miles. She tried again and hit the wall. A third tinkered against the glass door and clattered on the steps. Willa ducked down quickly out of sight, her heart rapping. There was no response. She was just considering whether or not to try again, when she saw the door slide sideways, and Louie standing there.

Willa slid through the ferns and slipped on the mud of the garden, then she was there, panting white breaths. Louie was silent.

"Hi," said Willa, suddenly stuck like clay to the spot.

Louie looked tight and pale, her eyes round dark shadows. "Hi."

"I just wondered—if you were all right."

Louie gave a weak laugh and looked desperate.

"Like, I don't know..."

There was a long silence while Willa felt the cold seep through her. Louie was quivering, she suddenly realised. Every time Willa met her eye, Louie would smile wryly, and shake her head, look to the sky, rub the back of her neck with a shaky hand. Her starling-black hair was flattened and dull, like a dead bird. In the end she said, "Willa—"

"Yeah?"

Louie shook her head again. "I'm okay. I just need . . . time out."

Willa felt her stomach contract. Time out.

"Time to think, to work stuff out. I'm not—" her voice was ragged and trembling. "I just never had time, you know? To think about it. It happened so fast, and . . ." she shrugged. "I don't know what I want."

Willa had stared at her, trying to understand, willing Louie to say the words she needed to hear. They never came. The words that came were horribly like ones she'd heard before. Judas lay down at her feet and Willa stared at him instead in silence.

"Please don't hate me," said Louie.

"How could I hate you?"

"I'm going to Bali, it'll . . . give me time."

Yeah, with your family, thought Willa. She nodded, and swallowed. "Enjoy yourself, eh."

Louie snorted and looked at her in such pain that Willa couldn't bear it. "I love you, Louie," she said, starting to cry though she'd promised herself not to.

"I know." Louie's voice sounded ready to snap in two. "I love you too," she said, at last, at last. "But that's not the point, is it?"

"Isn't it?"

They stood and looked at Judas for a bit, then Willa sniffed. "You know where to find me, if . . . well." She looked away and tried to stop the tears but it was too late. All the stress of the last few days caught up with her—and she wrenched herself away, stomped through the mud and ferns back onto the street and ran this time, ran with Judas beside her, and to hell with the ringing of her boots on the pavement.

All the way down the hill she choked on great sobs which were forced out of her every few steps. Near the bottom was a park bench and Willa skidded onto it, racked with sobbing. Judas nosed her hand worriedly, then jumped up on the bench to lick her tears. She buried her face in his fur and hunched over, crying.

She'd really believed Louie wasn't like Cathy. With Louie, Willa had thought there might be a future, a chance—she'd trusted her. But it was exactly the same. Sicko Willa, corrupting poor straight Louie. That's what her family would tell her, that's what Louie would believe, and maybe, maybe that was the truth?

# willa

Jolene knew something was up. She knew better than to force the issue, but when your daughter is crying herself silly in the next bedroom night after night, you can't ignore it. Often Willa didn't come home until hours after her shift was finished at Burger Giant. Jolene wasn't particular about that sort of thing—Willa was sensible—but the suffering in silence routine broke her heart.

Finally one night, she went into Willa's room with a pot of tea. "Here, this can't go on. You've got to talk about it, love."

Willa looked up in surprise. Had Jolene known all along?

"Did Mrs. Angelo ring you?"

She shook her head and laid the tray on Willa's desk.

"Oh. I can't talk, Mum," she whimpered. Then she cried again. "It hurts too much!"

Jolene wrapped her arms around her daughter and rocked her. "It always does, love. It always does."

"What's wrong with me?" Willa choked out.

"Nothing. There's bloody nothing wrong with you."

Willa pulled herself out of her mother's arms. "Yes there is! First Cathy, now... this. Why can't I just be normal?"

Jolene shrugged. "What's normal?" she smiled. "Anyway, same

106

thing happens, whether it's a boy or a girl. A broken heart's a broken heart."

Willa wiped her face with the tissues Jolene handed her. "You knew all about it, didn't you?"

"Look, I made a pot of tea. It's a flaming cliché, but it works. You never feel as bad after a cuppa." Jolene stood up and turned on Willa's bedside lamp. It immediately made the room warmer. Willa's clothes came to life, hanging along one wall from a wooden rod.

Willa blew her nose and took the cup her mother poured. Jolene fetched a woollen shawl and wrapped it around her daughter's shoulders.

"Now, what's that silly beatnik been up to?"

Willa told her. The bit about her and Louie in bed together when Mrs. Angelo came in made her go bright red.

"Oh god almighty," breathed Jolene. "You didn't do it there?"

"We weren't doing anything!" snapped Willa, then sighed. "Well, you tell me where we can go? I mean, there's nowhere, eh, just to be together."

Jolene bit her lip. "Guess not."

"And there are all our friends, with guys hanging out every weekend, every party— god! Just an hour together for us is almost impossible. Anyway, that's not the point." And she heard in her head Louie's voice. *I love you. But that's not the point, is it?*

"So, what now?" asked her mother.

Willa put down her cup and saucer and hugged the shawl tighter. "She needs 'time.' Which means she's changed her mind, just like Cathy." She sniffed. "Why?"

Jolene rubbed her daughter's shoulders. "Well, maybe Louie's not ready. Maybe she has changed her mind." Willa's heart sank. "But don't judge her too soon, eh? She only said she needs time. Give it to her."

107

"But her mother hates me. I'm not allowed to see her again!"

"Well, mothers can grow up too, you know." Jolene grinned at her. "I didn't like that business with Cathy." *That business.* "But then, I'd never had to think about it before. I hope I'm more understanding now, love. You know whatever happens, I still love you."

Willa brushed impatiently at the tears on her face, and nodded.

"Now, what about those blue letters."

Willa shook her head. "They're nothing to do with it."

"You sure? Sid reckons they are."

"Sid? You didn't tell him?"

"Well, who have I got to talk to, for godsake?" Jolene leaned sideways on the bed and pulled a cigarette packet from her dressing gown pocket. "He's my best mate. And that's all," she said, pointing the unlighted cigarette at Willa warningly.

"What did he say?"

Jolene flicked her lighter and dragged deeply. "Oh, just the usual. You could wring his brains out and be left with a lump of ear wax."

"Well, what?"

Jolene looked at her and rolled her eyes. "He puts it all down to raging hormones. Mind you, he's used that line on me, too. He's still looking for someone to blame. You're not his image of a dyke."

Willa reeled at the word. Her, a *dyke?*

"He's just a big lump, love. But he does care about you, and he won't say anything, I have his word."

Willa gave a weak smile. Great.

"Now," said her mother, getting up. "Do you think you might get some sleep? It'll do you the world of good, honestly."

"If you take that cigarette out of here."

# willa

It would have been better if it wasn't the holidays. There was too much time to sit around and brood. Willa took on extra shifts at Burger Giant, and strangely enjoyed her time there. Joan and Deirdre knew she'd "fallen out" with Louie and they'd decided that Louie was to blame. The main reason for their decision was Louie's being in Bali on holiday and Willa's working with them at Burger Giant.

Even Kevin was being nice to her now. He invited her out after work, and once or twice she went with him and Kelly to a mate's house to watch a movie, or to a bar. They made a big deal of her getting in underage, and Willa just smiled and wondered how they could think she'd find a pub glamorous. One time Keith turned up, so Willa left quickly.

Every day she collected the mail, hoping for word from Louie, and every day she was disappointed. She received two more blue notes. One said: *God sees everything*, the other, *I love you*.

Eventually, one afternoon, Cathy rang.

"Can you talk?" she asked. Her voice was thin and high, like a doll's.

"Yes," said Willa.

"There's no one around?"

Willa sighed. "No, Cathy, I'm all alone."

"I just wanted to tell you—I know it wasn't your fault."

"Oh."

"And I'm sorry. I'm sorry I blamed you for everything."

Willa stared out the window at the blue wintry sky, a drift of pale cloud like old underwear over the hills. "Yeah, well," she said finally. "Thanks."

There was a pause. "You know I still feel the same sometimes?"

Willa didn't answer. She knew.

"I just want to see you, to be with you. Most of the time I'm okay, but . . . I miss you, Willa."

"I miss you too." It wasn't really true, but so what.

"And . . . maybe you could come over?"

"I don't think so, Cathy."

Willa heard the tears starting, and sighed. This was such an old pattern.

"Please?" cried Cathy, her voice all whispery. "Not for long, Mum'll be home by five, but maybe . . ."

"No, Cathy. It'll only upset both of us."

Then she was bawling on the other end and Willa was trying to placate her, trying to reassure her she'd be all right. An hour later, when Cathy heard her mother's car in the drive, she finally hung up. Willa was exhausted.

It was a long, lonely weekend. She worked Saturday afternoon and studied at home the rest of the time, trying not to think of Louie. On Monday she got a card from Bali. All temperatures and places and Mum, Dad, Nic, Marietta. At the bottom she said *love, Louie,* but then, Mo would write that. Willa moped around the Duke trying to be useful and only getting under Sid's feet. There wasn't even any fencing on Monday night because of the holidays, but then Marcus rang and suggested she and Lucan and he get together for a practice anyway.

Willa met them at the gym and forced the poor guys into a

workout as hard as any they had on official nights. She beat Lucan twice then let him win since he'd started to sulk, and followed it with a long bout against Marcus which he won in the end. He took off his mask and grinned.

"Whew! What a marathon."

Willa had lain on the floor to get her breath. He sat down, watching her carefully, while Lucan pulled up the mats.

"You've finally discovered some aggression, huh?"

Willa liked Marcus. He'd been her first friend at fencing, and wasn't egotistical about winning, like Lucan. Mind you, she'd never beaten him yet. His dark hair was damp and messy and his upper lip shone with perspiration.

"I needed an outlet," admitted Willa. "Sorry."

"Don't apologise. You could win the open event next week if you're still that angry."

Willa wondered how she'd feel in a week. Louie would be back, but would she have heard anything? She couldn't even imagine getting through the next seven days.

"You wanna talk about it?" asked Marcus in a mock American accent. "Sorry, physics doesn't help much with communication skills. But I'm a good listener."

"It's too long and boring, believe me." Willa untied her hair and pulled a brush through it roughly. It crackled with electricity.

"Try me."

Lucan banged a cupboard shut and came over.

"Maybe some other time. Thanks," she said, as Lucan picked up their gear, stuffing it in a large canvas bag. He grunted something and disappeared.

"We-ell," continued Marcus, "speaking of some other time, the film festival's still on this week. We could go and see a movie, have coffee, you could tell me your life's problems...no?" he tailed off.

Willa put down her brush and bit her lip. Marcus was kind,

gentle, smart, he was even good-looking. But he wasn't Louie.

"I'm sorry, Marcus. I really like you. It's just—there's someone else."

He nodded. "The one who makes you angry. Lucky guy."

Louie got home on the Saturday before school started. Willa knew because she saw the lights on at the Metal Petal when she just happened to be walking Judas past, as she did at least three times a day.

She heard nothing. She stayed up, fully dressed and pretending to study all that night, in case Louie came past the Duke. She didn't show; nor on Sunday. With a stomach full of stones Willa went to school on Monday and saw Louie the moment she opened the door to the seventh form room. Willa was shocked at how thin and drawn she looked, despite the fresh Balinese tan. There were greeny-black rings under her eyes. Vika and Mo were congratulating her on losing weight.

"Hi there," said Louie carefully when Willa came in.

"Welcome back."

"Thanks. Hey, um . . . I've got Art History first thing," Louie pretended to look for something in her bag, "I'll catch you later some time . . ."

Willa steeled herself. "Don't bother."

Louie looked like she'd been slapped. The others were silent.

"Not unless you've got something to say. You've made yourself perfectly clear." Willa turned and left.

They didn't share any classes, and it was weird how little Willa suddenly saw of Louie. Before, it seemed she just had to walk down a corridor, or into the library, and there she was. Now Willa hardly saw her. Once she was in the canteen queue, too far away to speak, and once she was three rows away in assembly.

Then, one afternoon when Willa was reading in the library she spotted Louie outside. She was walking across the quad in her black jeans and beatnik coat; walking slowly, her feet dragging. As Willa watched, Louie paused at the professional cookery room and tried to look in the windows. When she didn't find Willa, Louie slumped against the plaster wall, and lifted her face to the heavens. It was enough for Willa. She leapt up and rushed out of the library, along the corridor and out the side door into the cold wind. By the time she rounded the corner, Louie was a distant figure heading slowly towards the school gates. Willa ran after her and was just about to call out when she noticed the sleek white Mercedes parked outside the entrance. She pulled up heavily and watched as Louie opened the door, got in and Susi drove off.

# louie

Food disgusted her. Just the thought of it made her stomach bloat and turn over, her throat tighten. When Susi put food in front of her, Louie stiffened and went grey. She nibbled edges of things, placed tiny pieces just inside her lips and tried not to smell or taste them. Susi started to make such a big deal about it that Louie insisted on taking her meal to her room where she promptly threw it out the door into the ferns. She could hardly stand having the dirty plate in her room afterwards, and took it back as soon as possible.

She felt sick most of the time. She really had been sick: vomiting and feverish for about four days after It happened. It was ironic; they nearly didn't go to Bali after all. In the end it was Louie's decision that they should. Anywhere would be better than the dark paralysis of her bedroom.

One good thing about Bali was that she could lie on the beach wearing sunglasses and cry without anyone knowing. Her parents left her alone, convinced that time, sun and fresh fruit would do the trick. Instead, she lay awake all night, lay in a stupor all day and stopped eating anything except oranges.

She looked at figures walking on the beach: beautiful men, beautiful women. She tried to find them attractive; first men, their strong legs and bulky muscles, their tight bottoms and bronze shoulders. She watched them dive powerfully into the crashing sea, she watched them twist at the hips stitching up the waves on their surfboards. Then the women; their long slim legs and neat waists, the flight of their hair, the sway when they walked. But she felt nothing. She failed both tests. All she knew was that when she thought of Willa, her flaming hair and small kind hands, the soft smell of her neck and the gleaming oyster-coloured skin of her belly, Louie's head swirled and she felt as if she were falling from an aeroplane. She would grip the sides of the sun lounger, take deep breaths and force herself to focus on something close up—a shell, a bottle of sunscreen, a coloured towel, and slowly, slowly, everything would stop moving.

She watched Nic, too. He surfed and sunbathed, he drank beer and chatted up women on the beach, he joked with everyone they met, played with Marietta, and charmed the staff at the hotel. Susi fussed over him and Louie noticed for the first time the look in her mother's eyes as Nic was admired by young women. It was pride, the pride she was missing out on with Louie, but it was something else, too. Louie noticed how Susi liked to touch Nic, drape an arm around him, ruffle his hair, pat his leg.

Nic was kind to Louie. He took her side once or twice when Tony and Susi tried to force her to join them for dinner or dancing or something stupid. "Hey," he'd said, "she's okay. She's just chilling out. Leave her alone." One day Louie walked with him into the market and bought fruit, earrings and a sarong. It was the best day of all: she liked being around real people, not the glossy hotel crowd. But that night she spotted a look exchanged between Nic and her parents, a pleased nod in her direction. How much did Nic know? The next morning at the beach she was silent again, and when Nic's quips got him nowhere, he snapped, "Get over it, Luisa. It's only a girlfriend." She heard her own scream as if it came out of the earth, and when she ran out of things to throw at him she heaved handfuls and handfuls of sand until she'd dug a hole that she collapsed into sobbing, the world spinning, the ground subsiding again.

The panic attacks continued when they returned home, but by then Louie could hide them better. The worst was when she first walked back into her bedroom. It had a smell—not of Willa, but of Willa and Louie and the room combined—which pierced her chest, turned her legs to dust and left her crumpled on the bed, gasping. In the end she threw open her suitcase and buried her face in the Bali clothes, in their spicy foreign smell, then opened the ranchslider to the bitter air and gulped deep breaths. Even the roll of the ranchslider was now Willa; the loamy smell of the ferns outside was her too.

The next day they all went to Sunday mass, and this time Louie found it vaguely comforting to recite the familiar prayers, to sing the familiar hymns, to be soothed by the careful deep voice of the young priest. He was wearing proper black shoes this time, no Reeboks, and when they stopped to speak at the church door there were no special words for her, no insight into her suffering, just a moment—did she imagine it?—when Susi mentioned the new school term and he placed his hand very, very gently on her shoulder. .

Louie dreaded school more than anything. The first morning her entire body shook while Mo and Vika gabbled around her. She knew the minute the door opened it was Willa.

"Hi there," she managed to force out.

"Welcome back." Willa's eyes were frighteningly blue, glittering.

"Thanks." Louie couldn't breathe. There was a roaring in her ears. She rummaged in her bag, then stuttered something about seeing Willa later and tried to escape.

Willa's voice slammed into her. "Don't bother." It was a heavy, dull sound. "Not unless you've got something to say. You've made yourself perfectly clear."

116

Louie couldn't remember anything after that. She moved from class to class, she filled up sheets of paper with writing, she pulled out books and put them away. She thought she had been silent throughout, but sometimes was surprised to hear her own voice chattering to friends, or answering a question in class. At such times she would stop bewildered until someone else filled the gap.

After a few days she found it easier to speak, to laugh, to play the game, but it never seemed real. What was real was the agony of glimpsing Willa in assembly, the cooking room, the cafeteria, and not being able to say or do anything.

On Thursday Susi picked her up from school early and took her to the medical centre. Susi stayed in the waiting room but Louie knew immediately that she'd already briefed the doctor.

Doctor Nolan was a small, fit woman with an expensive blonde haircut. She had a reassuring smile, and down to earth manner. Perfect.

"You've been having a stressful time lately," she said as she wrapped the dark sleeve on Louie's arm to take her blood pressure. Not a question.

Louie didn't reply.

Doctor Nolan pumped up the sleeve and made it prickle on Louie's arm. "Any problems at school?"

This was a question, but a leading one.

"Not really."

Doctor Nolan's mouth folded and she wrote down something, then ripped the velcro fastening and removed the sleeve.

"What about schoolwork. You've got bursary exams coming up haven't you?"

"Yes."

"And then?"

Louie shrugged. She didn't like this woman and her smooth professional manner. Doctor Nolan couldn't care less about Louie's future.

"I thought I heard something about law school?"

*So why do you have to ask me?* "Maybe," she answered, not looking at her.

"Hmm, law school's pretty competitive these days. You'll need to get good bursary results."

"It's the intermediate year that counts," Louie said, looking her in the eye for the first time.

"Really? Looking forward to that?" She was pretending to be reading Louie's file.

"I suppose."

Doctor Nolan smiled at her encouragingly. She put her finger on the file. "There's no mention here of contraception," she began and put her head on one side. "Are you sexually active?"

Louie was dumbfounded. She felt herself go bright pink. What could she say? If she said yes, the doctor would want her on the pill. But she didn't need contraception. And yet she was damned if she was going to say no.

Doctor Nolan came to the rescue. "I know it's not easy to talk to parents about sex. So whatever we discuss in here goes no further." *Oh yeah,* thought Louie. "Most seventeen-year-olds I know are sexually active, or thinking about it. Would you like to discuss different options for protection?"

Louie sat as far back in her chair as she could. "No," she spluttered, "no, I've seen it all in sex education classes. Thanks," she added.

"Are you sure?"

Louie nodded fast. "Positive."

"Okay." Doctor Nolan paused for a moment, then stood up and asked Louie to sit on the bed while she felt her glands.

"How's your appetite?" she asked casually as she pressed around Louie's neck.

*So Mum's told you that too.* "Not bad."

"Feel like eating?"

"Not much."

"Mmm. You've lost a bit of weight I think."

*What would you know? You see me once a year.*

Doctor Nolan took a leaflet from a shelf above her desk and handed it to Louie. *Eating Disorders.* "I'm not suggesting you've got an eating disorder Louise, but it's young women of your age who are most at risk. It's very important to nip it in the bud, because these things can take over and believe me, I've seen some very very unhealthy young women. And it starts because you're unhappy. You are unhappy aren't you?"

Louie felt the tears start. She ducked her head and nodded.

Doctor Nolan put a firm hand on her shoulder, not like Father Campion's. Hers said, You must get over it; his said, I know how it is.

"You've had a problem with a friend you're very close to, perhaps?"

Louie sighed. She couldn't beat this woman, she was too smooth. She brushed the tears from her face and nodded again, harder.

"It's very painful, I know." Her voice was soft, reassuring. "But it's perfectly normal. You must remember that. At your age there are so many hormones being released into your system that the body almost dictates that you fall in love. Your primary relationships are with your friends. Sometimes those hormones just kick in and turn it into something much more intense. It's not your fault, and there's nothing wrong with you. It'll sort itself out with a bit of time, believe me."

The doctor handed her a tissue and bestowed her best smile on Louie. *Good girl for crying.*

"I wouldn't be a teenager again for anything. It's hard isn't it?"

Louie wiped her face, hating that she'd gone along with all this. Willa wasn't a friend. Willa was never a friend. How could she put it all down to *hormones?*

"Just give yourself some time, some distance, try not to dwell on it, and it will go away." The understanding tone gave way to a firm command. "Focus on those exams, on your future, that's the important thing."

Doctor Nolan got Louie to take off her jersey and listened to her heart. "Well, it's not broken!" she announced with a bright smile, handing back Louie's jersey.

That was it. Louie looked at the doctor, so bloody sure, so I Know Best, and decided. She grabbed her jersey and pulled it on as she stood up.

"Thank you Doctor, for all your—advice. But I don't think this is something you can help me with." She opened the door and walked out into the waiting room, to be met by Susi's false, expectant face.

Susi lurched from understanding and concern to fits of exasperation over Louie. She wanted her daughter to get better but she was infuriated that Louie wasn't eating. It seemed to Susi a deliberate tactic to get back at her. Louie was equally confused. She could see the worry in her mother's eyes and she wanted to make it go away, but when Susi snapped at her to stop moping or eat something for god's sake or just pull herself together, Louie's anger was violent. She said anything, anything that would hurt her mother as much as she'd hurt Louie.

Tony, on the other hand, was characteristically easy. He treated Louie the same as ever, he played down the eating, and concentrated on jollying her along. Some of the time it worked, and she was grateful for that. Marietta, jealous of all the attention Louie was getting, tried not eating dinner one night too.

"Don't you dare," said her mother through gritted teeth, and when Marietta disappeared upstairs with Tony in pursuit, Susi turned to Louie.

"See what you're doing? You're pulling this family apart!"

"Well you know all about pulling apart, don't you," Louie flashed back.

"I did it for your own good, Lou, you know that."

Louie rose to her feet. "You did it for *your* own good, Mum. You were thinking of you, of the neighbours, of the church group—anyone but me. Don't give me that bullshit!"

Tony returned from upstairs and took control. "Both of you stop it." His voice was always quiet in an argument. "Suse, have a sit down." He handed her the remains of a bottle of wine and shepherded her into the living room.

"Now, Lou," he said, returning, "give me a hand clearing up."

"I don't want to." Tony stopped and raised his eyebrows at her. "Oh, all right." She hated the sulky sound of her own voice.

They cleared the table and stacked the dishwasher in silence.

"You have to forgive your mother," Tony said eventually.

Louie gazed at him. "I can't."

"What she said was true. She did the only thing she could at the time."

"Like hell!"

Tony looked at her openly. "The only thing she could think of."

"Well that showed a remarkable lack of imagination."

"It's not an easy situation for anyone. Not for us, not for you, not for Willa."

It was a shock just to hear him say Willa's name again. Louie turned away and closed the dishwasher door and turned it on. A soft whoosh began the cycle.

"I don't think I can do this, Dad." She still clung to the door.

"Nobody's asking you to do anything right now—except get well. Whatever you decide in the long run is your decision. Much as we'd like to, we can't make it for you."

Louie leaned against the bench in surprise. Did he mean...?

"But you think it's wrong, don't you." She ducked her head. "Me and Willa."

121

There was a pause while Tony drew in a long breath. "I don't know, Lou. I don't like it. And I don't like seeing you and your mother so unhappy."

"It was fine until she found out." But was it? Louie thought of how sick she'd begun to feel, how knotted up at church, how guilty that she was lying to everyone, and not spending much time with Mo or the others.

"You know, when I was at St Peter's I had a mate, Stevie Carmichael."

Louie looked up. Her father was walking towards the window, his hands in his pockets.

"I thought Stevie was the next best thing to the Pope. He looked like something off a toothpaste ad, he sang like Paul McCartney, and played rugby like a demon. And he had a car," Tony grinned, turning around so he was framed by the night lights across the valley. "A Citroën. Well, I followed Stevie Carmichael round like a flaming border collie for six months. We used to skip school and go to the pool hall down town, smoke those nasty Russian cigarettes and listen to Manfred Mann. When Stevie left school in the sixth form and moved to Dunedin I wanted to go too, I really did. Your grandmother had no time for him."

Tony made a pattern on the rimu floor with his toe. "I cried every night for a week after he left. I didn't know anything in those days, you didn't. But I had a crush on Stevie Carmichael all right." He looked up at Louie. "Do you know where he is now?"

"Where?"

"Round the corner in Tanner Road." Tony laughed out loud. "He was gay all right. He's a hairdresser in town, complete works, chains, bangles, camp as a row of pink tents. He's okay, I guess, but well, you know what I'm saying? It's easy to get caught up with someone strong-minded and make too many decisions too early."

Louie sighed shakily and her father came over and bent his head into her vision. He smiled hopefully. "Okay?"

She nodded.

"Promise?"

Another nod.

He waggled his eyebrows. "Ice cream?"

"Na."

"Worth a try."


Louie sat in her room and tried to think things through. Was this all about hormones? Was she just caught up with Willa because she was strong-minded? Was it right or wrong?

She picked the old dictionary off her bookshelf and looked it up.

"Lesbian: Of or pertaining to the island of Lesbos, in the Grecian archipelago. 2. Lesbian vice: Sapphism."

She flicked to the Ss. "Sapphism: (from the name of Sappho who was accused of this vice;) Unnatural sexual relations between women."

Louie's hands dropped. *Unnatural sexual relations.* She thought of how she'd felt when she first kissed Willa, compared with how she'd felt kissing guys. It always came back to that. It didn't feel wrong. In fact, it felt right.

She'd been avoiding looking at something else, too. To be fair to her father, she'd better face it. She walked back to the shelf and picked up the Bible.

# willa

It was a hot and steamy midnight at Burger Giant. There's a good opening sentence for my next creative writing assignment, thought Willa. The condensation ran down the insides of the windows and the noise rocketed about from vinyl floor to chairs, tables, seratone walls to plaster ceiling. It was such a harsh, clanging sound compared with the deep hubbub of the pub. Willa was hot too, and tired. Her wrists were sore from flicking closed the hamburger containers and putting orders into bags. She didn't see the customers' faces any more, they just became orders, totals and change.

Simone was serving with her while Kelly and the new girl, Rebecca, were clearing tables. They were flat out, all of them just hanging on until the night shift started at one. Finally, when there was a lull behind the counter, Simone stretched her neck and yawned.

"Why does everybody else have more fun than us?"

Willa grunted. "They're not having fun. God, why don't they all go home to bed?"

"There's still the Jimmy Barnes crowd. They'll be here as soon as the concert finishes."

In fact they started drifting in a few minutes later. Most were drunk and all were singing badly. They quickly took over the whole place, yelling to their friends, spilling drinks, throwing up in the toilets.

"Give me a five-year-old birthday any day," said Simone.

Kevin chucked a few out and managed to calm down the others, while Kelly flirted with the worst remaining table until one overexcited guy made a grab for her and pinned her against the wall. Kevin chucked him out too.

Then, thankfully, it was hand-over time. Poor Rebecca was only halfway into her shift and looked at them pitifully as they hustled out the back to get changed. The incoming staff were nearly all schoolgirls like her, except for Marty, a university student who was weekend night manager.

"Drink, girls?" asked Kevin, popping his head into the women's toilets. Kelly squealed and clutched her clothes to her chest in mock horror.

Simone rolled her eyes. "Josh is picking me up, thanks." Josh was her basketball playing boyfriend.

"Yeah, he's downstairs," countered Kevin. "We were just discussing where to go. He thought Retro."

Simone shrugged her acceptance, Kelly gushed and Willa said no. Then when Kevin had gone, Simone tried to change Willa's mind.

"Come on, come with us. Please?" she said making a face at Kelly, who had her back to them.

"I don't know. . ."

"Go on, Willa," joined in Kelly. "Retro's got great music."

Simone looked so desperate, Willa thought, why not? "Okay."

Retro did have great music and they let her in without asking for ID. Kevin was so pleased she'd come he kept shouting her drinks and Willa was so tired, she kept accepting them. Simone had an argument with Josh who refused to dance, so she danced with

Willa and Kevin. Kelly had picked up a builder with big hands and a house in Balclutha. Josh sat morosely at their table talking to two basketball fans who'd recognised him.

They really had nothing in common except Burger Giant, so it wasn't surprising that what conversation they had centred on work and the other people there. Simone kept exclaiming, "Don't talk about work!" but they kept on doing it.

At one point Kevin said to Willa, "So what have you done to piss Louie off?"

"What?"

"Louie. Louise. Luisa?"

"Yeah yeah. What about her?" Willa's heart was thumping in time to the music but her head was fuzzy.

"She won't work with you. Asked for separate shifts."

"Oh."

Kevin leaned towards her, his eyes bleary. "What did you do?"

"None of your business. We just fell out." Willa stared at the dance floor which was becoming a watery blur.

"I can see that." When Willa volunteered no more, he added, "I told her no can do."

"What?"

"Separating shifts. I can't carry on like that. So you'll have to make up, whatever it is. You're on together next Friday." Kevin fumbled in his jacket pocket. "Cigarette?"

In a daze, Willa took one and let Kevin light it. As she drew in, she thought of Jolene, and could feel her mouth forming the same shape as her mother's. She stretched slightly and leaned back in her chair like Jolene did after a drag, blowing out the smoke in a thin blue line. Then she reached for the glass of vodka with her other hand. It all felt very familiar somehow.

The next morning she couldn't remember anything beyond that moment. Jolene filled in some of the gaps: Kevin hammering on the Duke's back door at four o'clock, Willa throwing up on the stairs, Sid bellowing at Kevin for letting her get drunk, Willa crying and retching over the bath. She remembered a little of that bit, especially how cold she'd got.

Jolene was philosophical about it; she'd seen plenty of drunks, and said even kids who live in a pub have to obliterate themselves once before they learn. Willa remembered her mother hadn't been so cool about Bliss doing the same thing. Sid brought her some disgusting drink with egg and Worcestershire sauce which made Willa throw up again. It seemed Sid had stayed the night,

All day she moped in her room playing music quietly. Judas stayed curled up in the corner, his dark nose tucked under his tail. The worst thing was she had to work again that night on the five till one shift. Willa doped up on aspirin and arrived just in time.

Louie was there, finishing up. Willa closed her eyes and wished she didn't look so bloody awful. Kevin and Simone yelled out, "Hey, party girl! How're you feeling?" and laughed heartily. Louie gave her a funny look and Willa guessed she'd heard the whole story all afternoon.

She changed into her uniform and tried to act with some dignity, but the others couldn't wait to goad her as soon as she came in. Louie walked straight past without a word while Kevin said, "Keith Colling, eh Willa? Well, you're a dark horse."

"Keith?"

Kevin spluttered. "Don't tell me you don't remember!"

Willa turned quickly after Louie, but she'd disappeared. The room spun. And Willa did remember something about Keith. He was sitting beside her at Retro with his arm around her shoulders, talking earnestly and squeezing her upper arm. "Oh, god."

Simone was smirking as she took off her apron. "You were wasted, girl, really wasted."

"Tell me about it."

Simone just smiled and shoved her apron in the laundry bag.

"No, really Simone. Tell me." Willa lowered her voice. *"What happened?"*

Simone looked at her in surprise. "How much do you remember?"

"Dancing, sitting with Kevin and you guys, smoking a bloody cigarette, that was dumb, then . . . just patches. Keith . . . with his arm around me? Something outside . . . a taxi."

"You were chucked out, because you chucked up on the dance floor."

"Oh, god."

"That was only the start. Girl, you threw up everywhere. Outside the club, in the taxi—do you know how much that costs?"

Willa was dumbstruck.

"Hey, it's okay. Happens to the best of us. And Keith paid up."

Willa ran a hand across her face. "Keith."

"Yes?"

"I don't know what . . . I did."

"Ohh." Simone raised her eyebrows cheekily, then relented. "Nothing to worry about. He was keen, you were pissed. He was trying to kiss you when you threw up on the dance floor. I don't think he tried again."

"I can't believe it, he's such a creep."

"The best friend of our beloved leader?"

They laughed and Simone nodded in Kevin's direction. "He's your biggest worry. He wants to do it all over again tonight."

"Like hell."

Willa managed to get through the evening without being sick, but it was a battle. Just the smell of hamburgers made her stomach turn. Kevin put her on table duty, but that didn't help much. Half-eaten food was even more sick-making. Finally one o'clock came round and they handed over to the night shift. Kevin's invitations to party were only playful—he could see how awful Willa felt.

128

"Never mind, plenty of other nights. Keith won't be going anywhere."

Willa sighed. "Tell Keith to lay off, Kevin. I can't stand him."

"So you say, but your actions say otherwise." He chuckled and sauntered up the stairs to his office.

Willa untied Judas from the loading bay and walked slowly home. She couldn't remember ever feeling so tired.

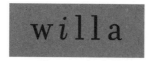

willa

She didn't hear from Keith all week, to her relief. Maybe Kevin had passed on her message. At school Willa was finding it increasingly hard to concentrate on anything. The only subject she was interested in was professional cookery, so she went to those classes, but she just couldn't face more than one or two other classes a day. She took off and walked Judas through the Woodhaugh bush for hours at a time, or went to movies in town. On Thursday she sat through the entire Star Wars trilogy next to a middle-aged teacher with a bad toupee who said he was wagging school too.

She'd seen virtually nothing of Louie all week, only Mo, who'd come to ask her what was going on.

"She doesn't want me around," Willa said.

"Why?"

"Hasn't she told you?"

Mo drew back her long dark hair. "You know Louie. She can't talk about anything that matters. She just looks in pain whenever I mention you."

"Her mother found out."

"Oh shit."

"And chucked me out. Louie hasn't invited me back." Willa stood up. "I don't know any more than that, Mo."

130

"Can't you at least talk about it?"

"It's up to her."

Mo sighed and folded her arms. "It's stupid. You two . . . well, you were really happy, even I could see that."

Friday at Burger Giant came around too fast. Willa had half-looked forward to it, half-dreaded it; in the end it was just more no-talks. Louie worked stony-faced out front with Deirdre while Willa served at the drive-through window. Even Kelly and Rebecca were quiet, working in the kitchen with Marty. Then at tea break Willa was sitting alone in the tiny staffroom when Louie came in.

She looked shocked to find Willa there, but walked stiffly over to a spare pink chair on the other side of the room. Willa found it almost unbearable to be so far away from her. After a minute or two, Louie broke the silence.

"Willa, I—um, I'm sorry about this."

"What in particular?" Willa heard her voice, hard and suspicious.

"Everything. Having to work together like this. I hate it."

"I'm sorry you feel like that." She did it again, and this time she saw the sting on Louie's face.

"I miss you." Louie's voice cracked and she looked down at the old newspaper she was holding. God, it was Cathy all over again. Willa hardened herself.

"And what do you want to do about it?" she asked.

Louie shook her head. "I don't know. I just need some space, some time . . ."

"Well, you'll miss me then, won't you." Willa couldn't take any more. She stood up and walked out, shutting the door quietly. As she stood there gathering herself, she heard an odd strangled sound from inside and knew Louie was crying. She wanted to go back in and tell her it was all right, but she knew it wasn't. It was the pattern she'd got into with Cathy, being rejected and then comforting her for doing so. This time she was going to protect herself. The knowledge that Louie was crying made her feel stronger somehow.

When she saw Louie downstairs later Willa turned quickly back to the drive-in window. It was cold work, the electric window sliding back and forth letting in blasts of freezing air, but Willa preferred it to the heavy smell in the restaurant and kitchen. Keith turned up and hung around trying to talk to her, but she froze him out until he gave up and disappeared. Finally it was knocking off time. Willa was just giving the money to Marty when Deirdre came in looking puzzled.

"Willa, there's someone on the office phone for you. She doesn't sound right. I'll do that," she offered, fixing the till.

Willa went upstairs to Kevin's office. It was Cathy.

"Willa, help me, please . . ." she cried.

"What is it? Cathy? What's happened?"

"Will you come here, please? I'm scared."

"What do you mean? Where are you?"

"I'm at the church," she whispered. "I . . . I don't want to die, but I need you, Willa . . ." and she started weeping in a high-pitched keen.

"Oh no, don't do anything silly, Cathy. I'll come."

"Will you? Will you really?"

"I'll come now, if you promise to wait for me — all right? All right?"

"Come quickly."

The line went dead.

Willa hung up and tore downstairs. She ran straight into Louie, putting on her jacket.

"Louie, you've got to help me. It's Cathy, I think she's going to overdose."

Louie looked back blankly for a second, then her face changed. "Where is she?"

"The church. Of the something or other saints, I know where.

God, god, god, I have to get a taxi." Willa turned to run back upstairs when Louie grabbed her arm.

"Dad, he's right outside, he'll take us. Come on!" She pulled Willa through the door outside and slammed straight into Keith, waiting in the carpark.

"Get out of the way!" yelled Louie, but Willa stopped.

"It's Cathy," she said to him. "You'd better come."

"What?" Keith gave a stupid smile, but Louie grabbed his shoulder and hauled him with her.

"Come *on!*"

The Mercedes was right there, its lights on, engine purring. Louie threw open the passenger door, screamed the news at her father and pushed Willa forward. "You get in the front, you know where we're going."

# louie

The car screeched around the corner and motored down the one-way system, through an orange light, swerved to the right and over the disused railway line according to Willa's directions until they lurched to a halt outside a pale blue building with a white cross.

"Round here," called Willa, running down one side. A light was on in the back room of the hall. Louie sprinted after her.

The side door was unlocked and they burst into the room where a small pale girl sat on a wooden chair. She was staring at the table where there was a telephone, a Bible, a bottle of Coke and several packets of tablets.

"Cathy!" screamed Willa, falling down beside her. "What have you taken?"

Cathy was so small and fragile, nothing like what Louie had imagined. Her tiny oval face turned to Willa and dissolved. "I didn't," she whispered and dropped her head so the blonde hair fell forward. "I didn't do anything wrong."

She was like a china doll, thought Louie, frighteningly break-able. Had she always been like that? What had Willa seen in her? Louie felt large and gawky suddenly, and tried to overcome her growing hostility to this girl. She watched Willa take a deep breath and turn to Tony and Keith. "She's fine." They both stopped, awk-

134

ward, unsure. There was an acrid smell in the room—old dust mingled with what Louie realised was Keith's sweat.

Cathy was sobbing silently. Her voice was a thin squeak and she grabbed Willa's hands. "I can't do it, Willa. I can't get over it."

"Cathy. . ."

"I try. I have tried," she said, looking up at Keith. "But I keep thinking about it. It's there in my head, all the time, and I don't know if it's me or. . . sometimes," her voice shook again, "I think I'm possessed or something."

Willa held Cathy's hands, and tried to rub some warmth into them. "There's nothing wrong with you Cathy, nothing at all. You just need to talk to someone about it."

"Come on Catherine," said Keith, stepping forward. His fair hair was cropped very short, and Louie noticed a red rash around his neck under the familiar collar and tie. "That's enough. We've gone through all this, and you have to be strong."

"Oh, for Christ's sake," muttered Willa.

"Don't listen to her, Cathy, she doesn't understand."

"Keith, she's a mess. She needs help." Willa glared at him, pain visible in her face. Louie wanted to leap in, grab Willa away from these people, but she was excluded, invisible in this old battle.

"She's got help," said Keith. "She's got her family and her church, and we're all praying for her. You've been doing so well," he said, his tone softening as he knelt beside Cathy. "You're just tired. You know you can do this, Cathy, please don't give up." Cathy buried her face in Willa's shoulder and began sobbing silently. Keith made an exasperated noise and stood up. "It's your fault," he said to Willa. She looked at him, her arm still around Cathy.

"You did this to Cathy. It's your fault," Keith repeated, his face flushing. "It's sick what you did. It's sick and wrong."

"It is not."

"The Bible says so."

"I don't care what the Bible says."

Louie was shocked. She looked from Keith to Willa as Cathy burst into loud weeping.

"Then you'll go to Hell," said Keith. "Don't you care about that?"

"I don't believe in Hell."

"Oh, *what?* That's just crazy. I suppose you don't believe in God!"

"No." Willa had stood too, let Cathy go.

Keith looked about him, his mouth slack. "Willa, you don't know what you're saying. It's evil, it's *sin,*" he said, his face suddenly contorting. Louie was surprised to see tears in his eyes as he advanced on Willa. "I know you're a good person underneath. I can help you change. Give yourself up to God and there's still a chance for you. For us."

Willa looked as if she'd been hit by a stone. She took a step back and stared at him. "It was you. You wrote those notes. It was you all along, wasn't it?"

"I only said the truth. You know that." Keith began pleading with her to let him help her, and his face was so desperate Louie almost felt sorry for him. Willa broke away and headed for the door.

"No, Keith," she said. "You're the one who needs help. Get away from me, leave me alone."

"I can help you, Willa," he was crying, but to Louie's relief Tony stepped forward and took Keith by the arm.

"That's enough. Calm down, Keith. *Calm down.*"

Keith shook his head and grimaced at Tony. "She's evil. Look what she did to Catherine. It's disgusting. She'll go to Hell for it, and she doesn't even care!"

"Don't be so stupid," said Tony. Louie watched her father, so small in his black woollen coat she thought, but so wonderfully sane. She could tell by his steady, cold voice how angry he was.

"What those girls did was love each other. Love is never evil in the eyes of God. Hatred is."

"The Bible says it's wrong, it does!"

"The Bible says a lot of things, Keith. And the most important gospel is love. Do you understand? Because your sister is sitting over there wanting to take her own life, and if ever she needs your love, it's now."

He steered Keith away from Willa and towards Cathy, talking quietly all the way. Louie caught Willa's eye but before she could say any of the million things racing through her head, Willa looked away and rushed out the door.

# willa

Louie had stared at her as if she was from another planet. Willa looked back in the small window and saw Keith and Tony huddled around Cathy. Centre of attention again. Sick Willa syndrome again.

Louie came towards her, hesitant. "Willa . . ."

*God, another needy voice.* "Go away, Lou."

"Are you all right?"

Willa rolled her eyes.

"Come on, you can't stand out here in the cold."

"I'm not going anywhere near that creep." She paused. "What are they doing?"

Louie looked through the window. "Coming outside. They're taking her home."

Willa snorted. "Till next time."

"Come on."

"I'm not going in the car with them." Louie began to protest, but Willa cut in. "Just leave me, will you? Just leave me alone!"

Louie went away, and Willa slumped against the concrete wall. It was freezing, but she couldn't get in the car with Keith—and she didn't want to be near Cathy, either. She wished she could just shrivel up and disappear. Then she heard neat clipped steps, and Tony appeared.

"You okay?"

Willa sniffed. "Yep."

"Listen, I've called you a taxi. It'll be here in five minutes. Will you be all right until then?"

Willa raised her head and met his eyes. He was such a nice man, Mr. Angelo, she suddenly felt like collapsing on his shoulder and bawling. Instead she grunted and looked away again. She felt him tuck something in her jacket pocket.

"You did really well, Willa. Cathy will be all right. And don't worry about Keith—I'll have a good talk to him."

"Yeah, thanks."

"You take care," he said, patting her shoulder, and then he was gone, the car doors clapped shut, just a drift of exhaust turning red as the taillights slid along the alley.

Willa gave them a few minutes, then began to run. She didn't want a taxi, she didn't want anybody. It felt like she'd been running for weeks. The sound of her boots' flat dinging on the pavement rang in her head and built up into a clanging percussion that made her temples hurt. She slowed down and heard her lungs wheeze, saw her breath puff out in white clouds. She was almost at Burger Giant.

Judas whined and squeaked at her, his claws scraping the asphalt as he jumped about. She let him off his leash and headed through the back streets towards the university area.

Eventually she found herself outside the fencing hall. Willa stood there for a bit and then moved on. She thought about Marcus, and that last training session when she nearly beat him. She smiled to herself—the open event he'd wanted her to enter was tomorrow—no, today actually. Willa's feet took her around the side of the Botanical Gardens to the house Marcus shared with some other fencers. There were no lights on there either.

She briefly thought about knocking anyway, and getting him up. Hadn't he said he was a good listener? Maybe she should have gone out with him. Maybe she still should. It would certainly please everybody, and he was a nice enough guy. Willa stood facing the brick terrace house waiting for a sign. *Come on,* she thought. *If this is what you want, show me. Turn on a light, open a window, shoot a star, whatever.* She wasn't sure who she was talking to—God, or fate, or Marcus? After a bit Judas started to sigh in his bored dog way, and Willa's feet got cold. She shoved her hands back in her pockets and started walking again.

It was a pretty dumb idea, but it was the only one she could think of. She turned left at the comer and trudged along a deserted campus street towards the Duke. It stuck out of the corner dark and silent like a big black tooth, a molar, Willa thought. Around the back Jolene had left the small outside light on for Willa, but her mother's bedroom was dark.

Willa slipped inside and down the hall. She lifted some spare keys from the drawer in the back room where Sid kept them. The alcoholic smell hit her as she turned the corner into the downstairs foyer. Willa didn't flinch. With a brief glance up the stairs, she unlocked the double glass doors into the lounge bar and felt her way around the tables and chairs. Behind the bar she took a bottle of whisky, slipped it into her big coat pocket and retraced her steps, locking the bar and replacing the keys in the drawer. She turned off the outside light as she left and led a puzzled Judas back out the gate.

The road that led to Signal Hill was long and steep and it was nearly an hour before the houses disappeared, leaving her alone on the narrow dark road she and Louie had driven up that first night.

Below her Willa could see the lights of the valley strung out in a lonely line. To her right Signal Hill rose up and shouldered her along the road, protecting her from the worst of the wind. It was bitterly cold though, and periodically Willa pulled the whisky bottle from her pocket and took short sips of the fiery liquid. It made her gasp in cold air and her mouth went numb. Judas weaved in and out of sight, the plume of his tail faintly visible in the gloom.

At one point Willa heard a car engine, and just stepped out of sight amongst the broom and gorse in time. The headlights rose above her and the car ploughed down the gravel road, skidding on the corner and enveloping the bush in a choking cloud of dust. It was a while before she located Judas and they continued on their way.

At the top the wind buffeted Willa almost off balance. She collapsed against the wall of the monument to catch her breath. She was alone, all about her the lights of the city, the roar of the wind, the sharp flicking of the long grass. Her eyes traced the streetlights below until she found the corner the Duke was on, and across the city to Cathy's house.

What was Cathy thinking now? Poor, sad, mixed up Cathy, who'd loved Willa, she knew that, but who couldn't love her too. Who saw a way out of it, a clean, easy, good way out. But being Cathy, she'd panicked and rung Willa. What if she hadn't? Would it have been better if she had died?

Willa used to know the answers to those questions. She was sure. Now, she wasn't. She thought of Keith, fantasising about her, writing those notes on blue paper, sending them to the Duke, leaving them in the letterbox, under the door, once even in her bag at Burger Giant. Creeping around watching her. Willa wrapped her arms around her head. It was too hard. Too horrible, too tiring.

And then there was Louie. It was here, what seemed like an age ago, that Willa had leaned over to feel Louie's cold ear, and couldn't move. The touch of Louie's skin had been an electric shock and Willa had frozen, feeling her heart skate across black

141

ice. She'd always remembered that moment. Now for the first time, Willa wished that she'd never done it, never leaned over and touched Louie Angelo.

She wished instead that she'd got some of those pills of Cathy's along with the whisky and could sit here, in the whirring grass and go to sleep, cold and numb, and never have to wake up.

Willa undid the whisky bottle and threw away the cap, as she'd seen Sid do when celebrating. She swigged a mouthful and choked, then recovered and drank some more. The lights below were blurry and distant, the earth she lay on seemed to move under her back, the grass clicked and whispered. At some stage she felt Judas lie down next to her and she dreamed her mother was beside her, wrapping Willa in a huge fur coat.

louie

Should she ring Willa? Dare she ring Willa? Louie brooded all Saturday morning, then decided to go for a bike ride to get away from her mother's prying eyes. Louie had heard her parents' voices talking long into the night, and knew Susi had been told all about Cathy, but so far that morning she'd kept her opinions to herself.

Louie rode her bike slowly, the thick tyres strumming the pavement as she freewheeled towards the Duke. She paused by the back gate, but there was no sign of Willa. With a woof Judas appeared at the gate, tail whipping the air in welcome. A minute later a human sounding sniff made her look up. Jolene.

"Hello Louie."

No more beatnik, Louie noticed. And Jolene looked . . . sad. There were lines around her eyes that made Louie think of old tragic movie stars.

"I was wondering if Willa was around," she said, patting Judas.

"She's not very well." Jolene looked at Louie carefully. "She only came in early this morning, a bit worse for wear. I thought she'd been with you."

"No. I mean, last night yeah, but . . . what do you mean, worse for wear?"

Jolene sighed and looked up at Willa's window, where the blind was down. "She's very unhappy, Louie, you know that. And Cathy, of course."

Louie nodded, wishing she was anywhere but here.

"Well, she can't carry everyone's problems. She thinks she can though, like I do, and like Bliss does. It's a weakness in the women of this family," she said and laughed. Then she waved a hand at Louie, "Don't worry, I'm her mother, that's my job. But hey, Beatnik," she fixed Louie with her light blue eyes, "you sort yourself out, I don't want no more Cathys, okay?"

"Okay."

"I'll tell her you came by. And thank your father for ringing, too."

Louie pushed off on her bike and headed up the valley towards home.

It was a beautiful day, that sort of fragile sunny day you get after a week of wind and rain. The bush was bathed in white sunshine except for the few patches of permafrost which Louie pedalled through tentatively. Native birds called in the stillness across the valley and it felt great to have the warm sun on her face again.

Through the dazzle of sunshine flared the spire of the All Saints Church. Louie found herself wondering what Father Campion did in between Sunday masses, and whether he wore his Reeboks or the shiny black shoes. She heard Jolene's parting words in her head and turned left into the church drive.

Round the back of the church was a small brick house where the priest lived. It had a stream running behind it. Louie leaned her bike against the front porch and rang the bell. When no one answered she walked around the back where she found Father Campion crouched over a clump of dead-looking plants. He was wearing faded jeans, a fisherman's knit black jersey and, yes, the shabby Reeboks.

Louie cleared her throat and thought how phoney it sounded. But it worked. Father Campion swung round and stood up, shading his eyes to see her better.

"Oh, Louie?"

She was pleased he didn't call her Louise, even though her mother always did so in front of the priest. "Hi."

There wasn't anything else she could think of to say suddenly, and Louie felt the familiar confusion choke her up. Father Campion crouched back down on his haunches. "I'm just cutting back these dahlias. They should have been lifted, I'm told, a couple of months ago, but I'm afraid I'm a bit of a garden-free zone, as they say. Father O'Leary was so proud of it, too."

Louie stood awkwardly. She knew even less about plants, and wondered if Father Campion was just going to ignore her. Her hands felt big hanging at her sides.

"There," he said, sounding satisfied. "Louie, would you be so kind as to wheel this lot round the corner to the heap for me?" He indicated a wheelbarrow filled with what looked like straw. "Just follow me." And he scooped up a pile of weeds and dead leaves in his arms and led her to an old wooden crate full of potato peelings and other muck where they dumped all the garden rubbish.

"Well then, I think we've earned a cup of coffee, don't you?"

Louie smiled at his kindness and went through the door Father Campion had opened for her. Inside there was a big old dining table with six chairs and a couple of armchairs. The priest waved at them and told her to make herself comfortable while he made the coffee. Louie chose one of the armchairs from which she could watch Father Campion working in the kitchen. He was a small man, neat in his movements, and he gave the impression of being quite athletic. He twisted from one bench to the other, crouched down to get something from the back of a cupboard and bounced back up. Louie imagined him in shorts on a soccer field and found the image quite possible. He'd look good in shorts she decided,

145

and he had an attractive, if not downright handsome, face.

Yet this man was celibate. A vow of no sex, ever.

The celibate man came through to the dining room and placed a tray on the table. As he poured her coffee he asked her the usual bunch of questions about school and family and the holiday in Bali. Then he settled in the other armchair and sipped from his mug.

"So, is there something that's worrying you Louie?" he asked softly, easy.

Louie tried to start at least three times before she got anything out.

"I wondered what you thought of, ah . . . well, what the Church's stance is on, um . . ." she took a deep breath, "homosexuality."

Father Campion contemplated his coffee for a few seconds, then fixed his eyes on Louie's. They were a dark brown. "Well, you've asked me two questions there, Louie," he said, carefully. "I gather this isn't an academic question."

"No."

"On the question of homosexuality the Vatican still believes it to be a sin, although the direction is to hate the sin and not the sinner." He paused, while Louie heard the words *sin* and *sinner* replaying in her head. "However," and his tone was much gentler now, "it is my view that the issue is more a matter of love, than sexuality."

Louie looked at him hard. "Love?"

"I believe that sex should be an expression of love. And that it is wrong to have sex without love. So my concern would be whether or not you loved this person."

Suddenly it was Louie and Willa, not an "issue." Louie swallowed and tried not to go red. "Yes," she croaked, and stared at the patterned carpet, "I love her." Panic washed over Louie as the word "her" came out and she looked quickly at the priest.

He regarded her with consummate stillness. "And she? Does she love you?"

"Yes, I think she does."

Father Campion smiled. "How wonderful."

Louie stared at him.

"How lucky you are, to love and to be loved in return."

This wasn't what Louie had expected.

"Tell me about her."

Louie took a deep breath. "She's . . . my age, smaller than me, red hair, blue eyes . . ." This wasn't Willa, it was a police identification. "*Light* blue eyes, they can look like—opals," Louie ducked her head in embarrassment.

"Ah, yes," murmured Father Campion. "Go on."

She started again. "Her name's Willa. I met her for the first time at Burger Giant. She threatened to . . ." Louie thought of the scene with Kevin and stopped with a smile. "She's strong." That was true. "When it comes down to it, Willa knows where she stands, on important things. I like that. She doesn't muddle like I do, she doesn't make a big song and dance about it, she just does it. She's sensible." Louie took a sip of coffee and noticed her hands were trembling. "She's got these small, white hands and . . ." Louie looked at the priest. "If I was going to act Willa, I'd think of her hands. Neat, and certain. Not full of gestures or fist-banging, but, well, surgeon's hands, cook's hands, pilot's hands, you know? You could rely on those hands." Louie remembered standing under the planes at the airport. "And she's a daredevil. A dear devil," she said to herself, hearing the words. "Sometimes she just looks at me as if she's—I don't know—waiting. Waiting for me to get to where she is."

"And where's that?"

"Where you're not beating yourself up about it all the time."

"Is that what you're doing?"

"My parents think it's wrong, my friends can't mention it, the doctor says it's a stage, the Church thinks it's a sin. Of course I'm beating myself up." She glared at him for a moment.

"What do you think?"

"I don't know!" Why did he think she'd come here? Louie wished she could just leave. He was starting to sound like a counsellor. "I just wondered what you thought," she mumbled.

Father Campion put down his coffee cup on the dark table. "What I think," he repeated, and paused.

"I think that love is a gift. I'm talking about real love, not infatuation or desire, although those are difficult enough. I'm talking about the joy of love."

By now Louie knew she was bright red. She could feel it prickling all over her face and neck. She sat still, out of words.

"I'll tell you how I feel." He leaned back in his chair and put his head on one side. "Filled, filled with joy, an unspeakable joy that at times I can hardly bear. I find it hard to remember what my life was like before I fell in love. I find it hard to believe that people can just go about their ordinary business, shopping at the supermarket, cooking their dinner, walking their dogs, without screaming for joy. Fulfilled. Uplifted. Special. Like little things don't matter, and I love everyone, and we're all so indescribably lucky." He looked back at her with a quirky smile. "Yes?"

Louie nodded again, dumbfounded. "You're in love?"

"I'm in love with Christ, Louie. Huh," he snorted, "I know that sounds a little odd, but it's exactly what it is. I am in love. It just happened, I never sought it, but I couldn't turn away from it. And, after all, Jesus, so we're led to believe, was a man, and if we believe in the everlasting spirit, still is a man. You could say I'm in love with a man."

"But not a real man." Louie grinned.

"Oh, he's real to me, Louie. He's just not three-dimensional.

But I suppose what I'm saying Louie, is that love comes in many forms."

"Yes. Except..." she paused to think. Father Campion's love was for someone, something perfect. "Except I feel scared. Terrified at times. Out of control."

"What are you frightened of?"

Louie had no doubt. "Losing her."

"Mm. Tell me, where do you think love comes from, Louie?"

"I don't know."

"Think."

She shrugged again. "There's a piece, by Marcus Aurelius," she looked at him carefully but his face was impassive. "Anyway, he says, 'It loved to happen.' It's like that, it just...happened. And I was pleased," she added.

"Marcus Aurelius, eh? The old stoic himself. Well, he wasn't usually one for overwhelming joy, but that's a nice quote, isn't it. 'It loved to happen.' Yes." He seemed to mull it over in his head and for a moment Louie felt he'd forgotten she was even there. Then he poured more coffee into his cup with a sigh.

"You see, I think love comes from God. And so, to turn away from love, real love, it could be argued, is to turn away from God."

"What about the Bible—you know, Leviticus and all that."

"Oh, you've been delving into Leviticus, have you?" He whistled. "Well, Louie, you'll know then that Leviticus also tells us not to cut our beards, not to wear linen and wool together nor to eat crayfish or frogs or snails. I'm afraid that if we adhered to Leviticus the entire French nation would be an abomination in the eyes of the Lord."

Father Campion chuckled and offered her more coffee, which she turned down. Then he leaned forward. "I wouldn't concern yourself too much with literal interpretations of the Old Testament rules for the Hebrews," he advised. "You have to decide about this relationship you're in now, in the twentieth century. Whether you truly believe it's a good and right thing, or whether you do not. And there is the question of hurting others. What do your parents say?"

Louie frowned. "They want me to change."

He raised his eyebrows in a silent question.

"I've tried. I think the problem is, I don't really want to. Nothing seems as important as Willa."

"Indeed. Well, I can't make that decision for you. Prayer and thought—honest thought, Louie. And time. But keep love to the forefront of your thinking. Love for Willa, but also love for your parents, and love for yourself."

Father Campion gave her a couple of books from his library, one called *Meditations on Love* and the other essays on the Old Testament that she didn't think she'd bother reading. The final one was a collection of *Peanuts* cartoons.

"You can get carried away with the heavy stuff," he explained. "And I always thought Snoopy had some particularly interesting metaphysical views."

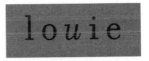

louie

Mo wanted them to do another Comedy Club performance to help raise money for the senior formal. At the mention of the formal Louie's blood ran cold.

"I don't think I'll be going to the formal," she said as they walked back to the common room with milkshakes and a filled roll.

Mo's mouth dropped open. "What?"

"Who am I going to take to the formal?" Louie asked, slapping her lunch down on a bench. Her appetite had got slowly better but there were still moments—like now—when the familiar gripe in her belly put her right off food.

Mo's face was like a tragedy mask "Oh, take your pick, girl. I know lots of guys you could go with."

"Maybe I don't want to go with a guy."

Mo looked blank for a moment, then the shock set in. "You're going to go with Willa?" she said in a whisper. Then with an incredulous grin, "You're going to take Willa! Far out!"

Louie slumped in a chair. "Unlikely. Even if I had the guts she probably wouldn't accept."

"Why don't you sort it out, Lou?"

"Can't. She won't speak to me."

Mo slurped the bottom of her milkshake. "So go with someone else. You can't miss the formal."

"We'll see."

It was good to throw herself into another Comedy Club performance though. Working with Mo was like remembering who she used to be, finding she still had the same skills, the same sense of humour, the same rapport on stage with her old friend. Each joke Louie devised and acted felt like a little piece of herself reclaimed. Each ta-daa! on stage felt like a stamping of the jigsaw back in place. It was the only time Louie felt happy, and real.

Occasionally she saw Willa at school, but they rarely said more than hello. At Burger Giant she wasn't sure whether to be delighted or horrified when they were on shift together. Some nights it was better than others. Louie sometimes asked Willa about Cathy, and then felt consumed with jealousy to hear Willa's answers. Willa told her Cathy was in therapy, but looked at Louie strangely, as if there was more to tell. Was Willa seeing Cathy again? She couldn't even think about it.

One thing was interesting: Keith had disappeared from Burger Giant. Kevin had a new four wheel drive, but Joan said he'd got it from a car sales across town—and Keith's name was seldom even mentioned.

Often Willa went out with the others after work, and Kevin liked to tell Louie that Willa was a "real party girl." She hated Kevin's smirk when he said that. Occasionally Louie smelt cigarette smoke on Willa after tea break, and once Louie went outside to say hello to Judas and found Willa having a smoke with Deirdre. Willa looked hard and tarty somehow, as she blew a line of white smoke and stared at her. Louie knew she was looking shocked and priggish. She stammered something and went back inside.

The formal got closer, and the pressure on Louie to go increased. Vika and Mo and Julie were all going in one party and assured her they had a terrific guy called Jeremy lined up for her. Lunchtime conversations in the common room revolved around it almost exclusively. When her mother saw a mention of it on a school newsletter she moved into overdrive.

"We'll have to go shopping, get organised, Lou. Do you want to buy a dress or get one made?"

"I don't know if I'm going."

"Of course you're going, don't be silly. It's the highlight of your year. I met your father at our school formal."

"Not that I was her partner," added Tony from the couch.

Louie sidestepped the issue and had a long, relaxing spa, trying not to think of Willa and the controversy they'd cause at a school formal. As she went back to her bedroom she overheard her parents talking in the living room.

"It's her decision," said Tony, quietly.

"Yes but she'll always regret it if she doesn't go."

"You can't make her."

"She needs a partner that's all."

"Suse, you know why she doesn't want to go."

There was a pause. Then her mother said, "I thought she was getting over that."

There was a rustle of paper and her father didn't answer. Louie's heart thumped.

"The doctor was very good with her you know," Susi continued. "She was sure she'd get over it."

"I don't think she is."

Her mother's voice rose. "What do you mean by that? That we should just accept it? Give up?"

"Look what happened to Cathy Colling."

Her mother made a snorting noise. "Louie's not like her. She's a poor little thing. Anyway, you gave them that free holiday, she might come right too."

*Free holiday? What?*

"The trip won't change anything, Suse."

"Oh don't say that, it's not true. Anyway, it was very generous of you."

Her father sounded exasperated. "Look, I'm just saying Louie might be the same. You can't just bury your head in the sand."

"Well, I'm not giving up yet. She needs our support and help. That's why this formal is so important. It just might be the turning point." She heard Susi sigh. "I wonder whether Carol and Don's boy is going. Stephen. He's a lovely boy. I might give Carol a ring tomorrow. . ."

Louie sped down the hall to her bedroom. This was disaster. Stephen Dingwall was lovely all right—a lovely druggie who supplied half the school and kept axolotyls in his bedroom. And what was that about Cathy Colling? Tony had been in touch with her family? Giving them free trips? That must be why Willa had looked at her so strangely when she asked about Cathy. Oh god, thought Louie, poor Willa. Both me and Cathy bundled off on a holiday to get away from her evil influence. *She must hate my parents.*

The next morning Louie told Mo she'd like to go to the formal after all, with Jeremy, if he was still free. Everyone was delighted. Susi told her to go downtown and pick out a dress of her choice, Vika and Julie went with her and they spent all evening trying on a multitude of garments. She chose a simple black dress with long elegant sleeves, and tried not to remember Willa telling her how great she looked in her mother's "little black dress."

They had to walk past Burger Giant twice. The first time Louie never turned her head, but the second time she couldn't resist it. Kelly was serving, and behind her Louie just caught a flash of red hair.

Jeremy rang her the next night. He was nervous and nice; he even managed to stutter out how pleased he was that she was going with him. Louie thought he would do fine; and after the formal she was definitely giving him the flick.

Three nights that week Louie worked at Burger Giant. After much angling, she still couldn't get out of Kelly whether or not Willa was going to the formal. Eventually Simone told her that Willa was going to Kevin's party on Saturday night, along with everyone else not on shift.

"Are you coming?" asked Simone.

Louie shrugged. "Haven't been invited. Anyway, I've got the formal."

"But this'll be really late, like after eleven," said Kelly. "It's an open party. Go on, it'll be a blast."

Louie smiled. "Maybe."

"Louie," came a voice from behind. "You've got to come, it's the party of the century." Kevin leaned against the chip warmer and smiled. "Bring your mates. The more the merrier."

Louie flicked close the flaps of a double cheese burger and handed it on to Kelly. "I don't think so, Kevin."

The days leading up to the formal were a complete waste of time. Nobody learned a thing at school, and every available second was devoted to discussion of Saturday night. Vika was having a party afterwards, Louie—incredibly—was offered the car to take them all, Mo had an argument with Dion who refused to wear a suit. Briefly Louie thought how awful the hype must be for Willa and others who weren't going.

But in fact, Louie was in for a surprise. When she, Jeremy, Mo, Dion, Jay, Vika, Julie and Geoff arrived at the school hall there, immediately ahead of them being introduced to the principal, was Willa. She was with Marcus, the fencing guy Louie had met once, and he was wearing a white tux.

Willa looked absolutely stunning. Louie felt her breath disappear at the sight. She was in a long green velvet dress, and had wrapped her hair in a black and green velvet band, so the red poured out the back in ringlets like flame.

"*It will flame out, like shining from shook foil,*" quoted Louie, overcome.

"Pardon?" said Jeremy, and when she didn't reply he shook hands politely with the principal and her husband.

Mo was instantly by Louie's side. "Are you all right?" she asked her.

"No."

155

"I didn't think she was coming."

Louie closed her eyes for a moment. "Neither did I."

"Oh, Louie."

"It's okay. I can handle it. I just don't want to have to speak to her."

Mo was wonderful. She was on one side of Louie all night, Jeremy on the other, but still Willa seemed to be everywhere. The dark green with the white tux looked so striking, and a number of people admired them. Louie tried not to watch, but there they were, laughing with Ms. Rosen, talking to people Louie didn't even know, dancing, helping themselves to supper.

Louie danced and talked with Jeremy, trying to distract herself, but she knew she was talking nonsense. Jeremy didn't seem real. He was every bit as nice as Mo had promised, which made it worse. She didn't want to be using this guy to get through the night, knowing she would never want to see him again, but every time she looked at him that's what she saw—someone temporary, almost cardboard, someone she could move around the hall as a sort of shield against Willa and Marcus.

Almost every minute Louie knew exactly where they were in the hall. Then, at one point Louie stopped dancing with Jeremy, stopped and stood in the middle of the hall gazing frantically around. Marcus was talking with one of the band, but Willa was nowhere.

"What's up? You lost something?" asked Jeremy, puzzled.

"Ahh—mmm," stammered Louie.

"Do you want to sit down?" He took her hand and led her towards some seats. At that moment Willa came through the door from the foyer and scanned the room looking for Marcus. Her eyes met Louie's and Louie thought she'd never felt so desperate before in her life. She gazed at Willa, begging her to do something, come over and take her away from all this, but Willa frowned and looked the other way. Jeremy was trying to steer Louie into a spare seat he'd found, and she followed him, her vision blurring with tears. *God, I can't cry now!*

156

While Jeremy was getting her a juice, and Mo was trying to distract her with some story about Dena Mason's boyfriend Greg being thrown out, Louie followed Willa's every move. The band started up a slow number and Louie watched as Marcus asked Willa to dance. *Say no, please say no.*

They moved onto the dance floor. Marcus had his arm around Willa's waist, he held her close, his face against her hair, talking. One hand held hers, the other rested on the base of Willa's back and began to slide back and forth very slowly. Louie fixed her eyes on it, feeling every touch through her whole body. She didn't even hear Jeremy ask her to dance.

"Come on, Lou, we'd better go." It was Mo. "Lou," her voice was stern.

Louie looked up. Mo was standing in front of her, but all Louie could see was Marcus's hand on Willa's back.

"Let's go."

Jeremy was standing too, looking at her oddly.

Mo took her arm and pulled her quickly through the foyer to the toilets.

"You've got to get out of here, Lou. You're going to lose it."

Louie felt the tears begin.

"No, don't cry! Don't, please." Mo grabbed a tissue out of her sleeve and dabbed at Louie's face, then enfolded her in a hug. "It'll be all right. Let's just get away from here, eh?"

A couple of other girls were looking on, interested. One of them gave Louie a particularly sympathetic look and said, "Hey, listen, guys just aren't worth it, you know?"

Louie nodded dumbly at her, then looked at Mo and they both burst out laughing. Once Louie had started she couldn't stop the mixture of laughter and tears, and the two other girls lifted an eyebrow at each other and walked out. Louie and Mo collapsed into further hysterics. It was a long time before Louie could control herself enough to actually blow her nose, then Mo helped fix her make-up, they found their coats and bags and headed back out to the others.

"I don't want to go to Vika's party," Louie confessed to Mo.

"That's okay. But can you drop us off there?"

"Sure." Louie paused as they reached the foyer. The dance was finishing and people were already pouring out of the hall. "But what about Jeremy?"

Mo paused with her and scanned the crowd. "Hmm," she said after a moment. "That problem might solve itself." She indicated to their left. Jeremy was leaning against a wall talking animatedly with Dena Mason, who was beaming back to him at about a thousand volts.

"Oh, Louie." Jeremy smiled nervously when they appeared. "I wasn't sure where you'd got to. You know Dena, don't you?"

Louie and Mo nodded and Dena smiled sneakily.

"We used to be in the same cross-country team," Jeremy continued. "Um, Dena says there's a party at her place now. Do you think...?"

"You're very welcome to come," Dena invited them smoothly.

"Thanks," said Louie. "But you know, Jeremy, I'm feeling a bit tired. I'd rather just head home now, though if you want to go on to Dena's, that's fine. Honestly."

Jeremy looked extremely awkward. "Well...umm..."

"I mean it," Louie assured him. "I'll give you a lift if you like."

"I can give you a lift," offered Dena. "There's plenty of room in my car."

Jeremy looked from one to the other and decided not to angst. "Okay," he shrugged, accepting Dena's offer. "If that's okay with you, Louie, it'd be sweet."

As they left Louie saw two things. One was Jeremy heading towards the official photo corner with Dena Mason; the other was Willa huddling under Marcus's black greatcoat as they hurried across the carpark in the rain.

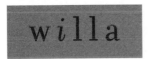

# willa

Music was already blaring from the old villa on the hill. The front door stood open to the rain, as did the windows, and people were standing under the shelter of the wide verandah, talking, drinking, dancing. Yellow light spilled onto their faces and Willa thought they looked ghoulish.

Inside it was all faces, bodies, cigarettes, glasses, bottles. The music thumped into Willa's ears and she could feel the heavy vibration through the floor, the tinny ringing of the walls. She spotted Kelly and Kevin and they waved. Kevin looked bleary-eyed already.

Marcus found them a spot on some floor cushions and Willa reluctantly joined him. This was the bit she had been dreading most, especially since it was the bit Marcus had looked forward to most. He handed her a can of beer.

"Here's to your one and only school formal," he toasted, then tore off the tab with a phiss.

Willa took her time drinking the bitter liquid, thinking if she kept the can at her mouth, Marcus wouldn't be able to kiss her. Then she lit a cigarette on the same premise. Kevin paraded past them with Kelly blissfully in tow.

He yelled something at Willa over the music. She couldn't

understand it. The third time he repeated it right into her face.

"Ya happy?" he screamed. His breath was hot and foul-smelling. Willa nodded to get rid of him. He winked and gave Marcus the thumbs up.

Willa tried to get Marcus to join others dancing in a separate room, but he wouldn't go. She suggested it would be quieter outside on the verandah, but he didn't want to lose their seats. In the end she gave up and let him kiss her. It wouldn't be too bad, and if she let him do it for a while she could go home.

What she hadn't counted on was the effect of another person's mouth on hers. As soon as their lips touched, Willa thought of Louie. Her head was filled with how different Marcus felt; how rough his face, how dry his lips, how big his tongue wallowing in her mouth. For a moment she had to fight off nausea, then she screwed up her eyes and concentrated on getting through it. It was quarter to one; Willa reckoned by one-thirty she could ask Marcus to take her home.

Whenever she couldn't bear it any longer, she pulled away, smiled at Marcus and took a breather. She smoked several cigarettes and opened but didn't drink about four cans of beer. If she saw Kelly or Simone she desperately tried to engage them in conversation but sooner or later Marcus would draw her close again, and plant his mouth on hers.

She guessed it was about one o'clock when it happened. Willa was just thinking she could go to the loo for a while and crib a few minutes, when she heard a disturbance. Pulling away from Marcus, she opened her eyes and saw Louie standing in the door opposite, dripping with rain.

Kevin was beside her, smiling and pointing at Willa but Louie didn't seem to be listening. Her eyes were fixed on Willa, her face a death mask.

Willa froze, staring back at her. Louie was still in her black dress, covered by a shabby duffel coat she'd got somewhere, which was heavy and sodden with rain. That and her wild expression made her look strange, a bit crazy. Louie's eyes moved slowly to Marcus. Then her face went ugly and distorted and she stormed across the room yelling something, pushing a woman out of her way. Marcus and Willa stood up together and Willa opened her mouth to say something but nothing came out. It was too late. Louie reached them, screamed at Marcus, grabbed him, shoved him, and he fell over.

Willa heard herself yell out Louie's name and then there was a general commotion. Someone tried to grab Louie, Marcus was jumping up off the floor, Kevin was smirking stupidly in the background. Willa met Louie's eyes, streaming with rain and tears. "I can't believe you'd do this," Louie said, then shook herself free and ploughed back through the crowd.

Willa turned to Marcus who appeared to be more mystified than hurt, and opened her mouth to explain. But there was nothing she could say to Marcus, not now. There was just a huge dragging sensation in her stomach as if it was ripping apart.

She dropped her cigarette in an empty can and said simply, "I'm sorry, I'm very sorry," and she stumbled through the people and out the verandah after Louie. Somebody yelled, "Where the hell's she going?" then a door slammed on the pumping music.

It was pouring with rain. It splashed into Willa's hair and face and she knew she was already shivering, although she didn't think of the cold. She looked up and down the steep winding road and saw no sign of Louie. She didn't even know whether she'd driven there or was on foot. Willa began running down the hill anyway. If she had to she could run all the way to the Metal Petal, and to hell with Susi and Tony Angelo. She ripped off her high shoes and ran in bare feet down the road. The loose metal cut into her feet, but the pain felt good and she ran faster, rain pelting into her velvet dress.

There was a gully on one side of the hill, houses banked up on the other. Below, the lights of the city jittered to Willa's running. The road wound like a dark wet snake up, down and back on itself and felt to Willa like a journey in her head through the past few tortuous months.

Around a sharp bend she saw a cloud of white mist rising up from the gully. She was almost out of breath and pulled up to a stop. Then she saw it—the lights of a car, flaring up from the bush. The cloud wasn't mist, it was exhaust, exhaust from the still running engine of a white Mercedes.

Willa plunged down the bank, ripping her dress on branches and grabbing gorse that tore her hands. The car was standing on end like the prow of a sleek white boat thrown up by the land. Things moved in milliseconds. Willa remembered snatching at doors that wouldn't open. She could see a shape inside. She was banging both hands on the roof in frustration, then she was banging on a front door and a woman in a floral dressing gown was looking at her. She saw men, torches and Louie, being pulled, so slowly, out the broken windscreen and all around them white steam lit up by the torches as if they were standing on a cloud watching Louie going to heaven. She was sticking her fingers down Louie's throat and wiping blood from her face, black sticky blood. She was gently removing a sliver of glass sticking out of Louie's cheek. The glass pulsed red, so did the bushes and someone said, "Thank God, they're here."

Then she was at the hospital, and people were talking to her. The words bounced off her randomly though she tried to catch them one by one. Nurses were trying to take her away and she fought. She looked down at Louie on a bed. Louie looked back at her and tried to speak. She was alive.

Willa was sitting in a small room with people she didn't know, when a priest walked in. He had soft brown hair and dark eyes and sat down beside her.

"You must be Willa," he said, touching her shoulder.

"Yes."

"I'm Father Campion, Louie's parish priest. You know she's going to be okay, don't you?"

Willa stared at him.

"She's out of X-ray and they had to fix a few broken bones, but there's nothing internal."

*Nothing internal.*

"Nothing wrong internally, I should say." And he smiled. "She told me about you. Described you perfectly."

"Can I see her?"

He nodded. "The doctor said she was asking for you. Willa," he said, as they stood up, "her parents are there too."

Willa frowned and walked with the priest along the quiet corridor to the room they'd put Louie in. She could hear his footsteps but her own feet didn't seem to touch the floor. She looked down and noted absently that her feet were bare and swollen, covered in cuts.

They turned through the door of a small room and Willa saw Tony and Susi first. Tony stepped across the room and enveloped her in a hug.

"Willa, thank god. Thank god you found her. I'm so sorry," he said and his voice went croaky. "I'm so sorry about everything." He gripped her harder for a long moment then released her. "She would have suffocated if you hadn't got her tongue out of her throat. I can't believe it, she could have been dead."

Susi had tears rolling down her face. She looked so miserable that Willa went to her and wrapped her arms around the woman who just cried and cried. Over her shoulder Willa saw Louie, lying peacefully, a plastered leg in traction and bandages round her shoulder and one arm. Susi let go and Willa walked over to the bedside.

"They've given her something to make her sleep," said Tony. "She was asking for you, but..."

Willa leaned down and touched Louie's hair, the black curls that sprang back into her hand, teasing. One eye was bruised and swollen, puffed up as if some red and purple creature was growing underneath it, and there was a row of neat black stitches like a zip down one cheek. Willa examined the nick in her other cheek where she'd removed the tiny spear of glass, and marvelled at the tracery of veins in her throat, her pale shell-like ear and the tiny moving pulse below it. She was alive.

Willa sat there for a long time, thinking. How she'd nearly lost Louie. How hard she'd been on her. She remembered the priest and wondered how much Louie had said to him. And who else? If only Louie'd been able to talk to her.

She cried then, dropped her head onto the bedclothes and felt the hot, wet tears soak into the sheet. There were arms around her shoulders, and someone rubbed her back, but Willa could only think of all the tears she'd cried, Louie had cried. Eventually, she raised her head again and wiped her face with a velvet sleeve.

"It was too hard," she whispered. Tony Angelo had tears in his eyes, too. "Too hard."

# willa and louie

It rained for two weeks. The drops bounced off the ground on the road outside Kevin's flat, and bounced off the beer cans still lying in the front yard. Rivulets gathered and flowed off the gravel road and down the bank where Louie had crashed the car, forming a muddy pool in the dent left in the bush. In town it drained into the softening earth and fed the roots of trees that were beginning to sprout red tips on their branches and it collected in the grey-green cones of tulips and daffodils that were budging through the soil.

The rain worked its way through the iron roof of Burger Giant, ran down a wall stud and filled up the powerboard until it short-circuited, plunging the shop into darkness. Deirdre took it upon herself to shut the doors, turn the main and tell the electrician to wait till morning. It dripped all night onto Kevin's desk.

At the Duke, Jolene put buckets and pots under the leaks in her bedroom and the kitchen. The water ran over the edge of the spouting just above the lounge bar door and the customers complained so much that she sent Sid onto the roof in the pouring rain to fix it. Willa cooked flat out in the kitchen to keep up with the demand for hot meals and Judas flopped in corners yawning and sighing at the boredom of it all.

From the Metal Petal Susi enquired about the cost of installing a free-standing designer fireplace and ordered long woollen curtains for the living room. Periodically she leaned in the doorway of Louie's empty bedroom and stood there thinking.

And at the hospital, Louie hobbled across the ward on her crutches, cracked a joke with the nurse and followed her father down the lift, across the foyer and out the main entrance doors. At the feel of the rain on her shoulders Louie smiled, lifted her head and closed her eyes, letting it patter over her face. Then she swung forward into the rocking gait that was becoming so familiar, and headed for the taxi.

That first day Louie spent re-orienting herself, resting, and discovering that crutches slip on polished wood floors. She listened hard to the speech her mother so painfully delivered and looked dutifully at the school work she had to catch up on. She even ate the whole helping of roast chicken and salad her mother gave her for lunch, although she'd lost so much weight in hospital, it was hard to fit it in. When Willa finally arrived, the rain had stopped and the world seemed washed clean. The sun shone in a clear blue sky, the hills tingled with green, birds darted amongst the trees. The flax outside Louie's door was shiny and sharp-edged in the sun and she watched a tui dip into a pottle of honey water.

They had spent plenty of time talking at the hospital since Louie's accident, but they hadn't been properly alone together since the night Susi had discovered them. Willa was more shy than Louie.

"I feel like we're back to square one," she said.

"Weird, eh."

"I'm scared to touch you in case it hurts."

Louie didn't answer for a while. She stared into the distance and then said, *"A coward dies an inch a day, a hero is quick dead."* She smiled at Willa. "It's a poem."

"Really."

"I read it in hospital."

"You certainly tried your best to be a hero, then."

"You were the hero." They looked at each other for a moment. Louie picked the carpet. "I was cowardly, Willa. I know that."

"Don't."

Willa noticed the dark circles under Louie's eyes when she looked down. She was so thin it scared Willa, but she knew better than to start in about the eating now. *Give her time,* she thought, *time to like herself again.*

"I memorised something else, listen," said Louie. *"What need have you of the black tents of your tribe, who has the red pavilion of my heart?"*

"It's beautiful."

"Tribal. That's what's been happening. I have to give up the black tents."

They sat for a while, silent. The tui ducked, listened, piped a green song into the air and flew off.

"Dare truth or promise," said Willa.

Louie grinned. "Dare."

"Come out to dinner with me."

"Dinner?"

"You, me and a restaurant." Willa paused. "A date."

Louie twiddled the bare toes that stuck out the end of her plaster, smiling to herself. Then she turned to Willa. "You're on."

They chose a small Greek restaurant above the city with open fires and small candlelit tables. *"Très romantique,"* said Louie, stomping across the floor on her crutches, nervous, obnoxious. Willa handed a bottle of wine to the waiter.

"You're not allowed to drink, you're underage," said Louie.

"Your father gave it to me."

"What?"

Willa laughed. "Tony gave it to me as we got into the taxi. Try not to think about it."

"Good grief. Any other secrets you have with my parents?"

Willa sat down and wondered what to say. It wasn't really the right time, but...

"Well, your mum had a word with me," said Willa.

"Worser and worser. What did she say?"

Willa looked at Louie straight. "Stuff about giving you time, exams, other interests... you know."

"Oh god."

"It was okay. She also said I was free to—how did she put it?— 'form whatever relationship we decide upon together.'"

Louie spluttered and her neck flushed. "I think she practised that one. I got exactly the same phrase. Along with the sex one."

"The sex?" Willa's voice rose and they both cringed, glanced at other diners.

"She doesn't want to know about it, basically," whispered Louie.

"Thank god!"

They sat still for a bit, embarrassed, until the waiter brought the wine. "At least this'll be good," said Louie.

It was. They drank the wine and ate the food—Louie pretending she didn't notice Willa watching her plate carefully—and talked about all the safe things: school, Mo, Julie, Vika, netball, music, Burger Giant, what to do when you get an itch under plaster. Louie played to the gallery, asking the waiter for a kebab skewer to scratch her leg with. He, no stranger to dinner comedy, presented her with a flaming skewer to the delight of the kitchen staff and other diners. The byplay continued over a doggy bag for Judas, which was promised in return for a dance. Louie took up the challenge and said she would pose on the dance floor like a Greek statue, since she was plastered in both senses of the word, and the waiter danced around her to general applause.

She wasn't drunk, as Willa knew. She just had to wind down.

168

Willa waited, amused, enjoying the entertainment, enjoying Louie's glances to make sure Willa was watching. Over coffee Louie relaxed, drew herself into the scope of their one table. They talked a little about Cathy.

"Trust Dad to think a free trip would fix everything," snorted Louie.

"That wasn't all he did. Cathy said he talked her parents into letting her go to a therapist. Mind you, I think she's getting obsessed with her therapist now."

"Poor Cathy." Louie paused. "Was she always like that?"

"Like what?"

"You know—all *pensive thought and aspect pale, melancholy sweet and frail.* Sorry," she added, awkward.

Willa shrugged. "It's okay. I just still can't believe you can do that. Find words for things."

"Only some things."

Willa thought about Cathy. "Yeah, I guess she was always intense—but I kind of liked that at first. Dumb, eh."

"Did you love her?"

Willa sighed. "I thought so. I don't know." She looked up. "Not like you."

Louie stared into Willa's opal eyes and thought how she loved her so much it hurt. "You looked so beautiful at the ball," she said, shaking her head. "I wanted to kill that guy."

"I thought you were going to."

"No. I realised in time who it was I wanted to kill."

Willa swallowed. "Did you drive off the road deliberately?"

Louie tried to remember how it had happened. The wild drive, the wet, the desperation. "Sort of," she said, not wanting to scare Willa. "It was a type of madness."

Willa reached across the table and touched Louie's face. "So," she said, "dare truth or promise."

Louie quickly glanced around the restaurant. She was going to

169

have to get used to this. She took a deep breath and closed her eyes. "Promise."

There was a long silence. Willa's voice ran through her like warm wind. "Promise to love me, Louie Angelo."

Louie's lips spread in a slow smile. "I promise."

Willa's hand traced her neck and faded. Louie opened one eye and looked at Willa wickedly. "My father didn't happen to slip some money into your pocket for a cheap hotel room by any chance did he?"

"Afraid not."

"An expensive one?"

Willa shook her head. She was stroking Louie's wrist now, a light, cool touch that was driving Louie mad.

"Then I'd have to say my mother is right on another thing."

"Which is?"

"It's not easy being gay."

"She said that?"

Louie grinned. "I asked her if she was going to break into song."

"What did she say?"

Louie raised her eyebrows coolly like her mother and mimicked her voice. "'I wouldn't go that far.'"

Upstairs at the Metal Petal Susi sat reading a magazine, trying not to think about what Louie and Willa were up to. In the garage, Tony inspected his newly repaired and painted Mercedes and patted the steering wheel in relief. At the Duke, Jolene was confiscating a plate of chips Sid had helped himself to. Cathy was writing a long letter to her therapist; Keith was sitting in a café watching a small red-headed girl wipe the tables. Kevin was trying to find an important memo from head office in the piles of papers drying on his office floor; Joan was laughing like a drain at Kelly's joke. And if anyone had been looking, they would even have seen Deirdre smile at the picture of herself as the Burger Giant's Employee of the Week.